Bellona: Book 4

Carbon Heart Silicon Soul, Volume 4

Jason Blacker

Published by Jason Blacker, 2019.

This is a work of fiction. Similarities to real people, places, or events are entirely coincidental.

BELLONA: BOOK 4

First edition. September 19, 2019.

Copyright © 2019 Jason Blacker.

ISBN: 978-1927623879

Written by Jason Blacker.

Kung Fu Fighting

Sheeba didn't use up all of the Anigloo. She hadn't asked Shad if she should. She had eyeballed it. It was too late now to confirm. She had to move ahead and replace the E3C. It looked right. It looked like the right amount that she had used on her successful trial runs. They were running out of time. It was now or never.

She lowered the E3C towards its bed. Sheeba was holding her breath. Please, please, please, by all that Fortuna holds dear, give me this one win, she thought. The E3C slowly made contact with the bed. She released the tool from the E3C and pulled it away.

"Is it right?" she asked.

"I don't know yet. It'll take a few seconds. Put the HEART back on anyway. We can't redo it," said Shad.

"Ten seconds," said Clarity.

"Shit," said Shad.

"Mars dammit," said Ny.

Rak sat and watched his wife grab the EEK and HEART and quickly and steadily place it over the E3C. It mated itself to the E3C and the EEK melted off. Sheeba's job was now complete.

"Five seconds," said Clarity, anxiety thick on her voice like a hot potato.

"Uploading LAZARUS," said Shad, looking over at Ny. "Perfect job on the E3C, Sheeba."

LAZARUS would need seven to ten seconds to upload and then Eve would automatically start the reboot which should only take three to five seconds. But under these circumstances that might as well be years. Shad took a quick tug on the tentacled wires. They were attached like glue to Eve's head. They should survive the harsh stopping of the van and complete the upload. Shad was glad for that. It was also the last thing he did before Mercury's Caduceus rolled through and over them like an electrified tsunami.

They were all knocked unconscious before Mr. T was flipped on its side. Clarity, in the driver's seat banged her head against the side window as Mr. T flipped over and slid towards the side of the road on the driver's side.

Shad landed in an awkward spot like a crumpled ball of human being with Rak partly overtop of him up against the side door. Ny was tossed to the left of Sheeba, landing between El who was still strapped into the hammock and the sidewall of the van, hitting his head on the cabinet that had at one point held the tools that Sheeba had used. This caused a gash over his left eyebrow that started bleeding eagerly. His air scrubber tore and sort of melted off his face.

Sheeba was the luckiest of them all on account of her being in a harness. She ended up semi-horizontal, floating over El like a fairy godmother, her shins resting on the edge of El's hammock over El's left arm.

Ny was the first one to regain consciousness on account that banging his head up against the cabinet startled his brain. He reached for the wound tenderly with his right hand and withdrew it when it felt wet. He saw the blood on his fingers which he wiped off on his shirt. He looked around for El's chest plate and scalp. They were both behind him in the corner of the van by the back doors. He couldn't reach for them. He was dazed and unaware his air scrubber had come off. The air quality in the van was almost as good as the outside on account of the additional sealing Shad had done to soundproof and make the van impenetrable from the jackboots.

He got himself to kneeling and reached up towards El. He undid her right arm strap as she rebooted. The wires from Shad's P-Mac fell off her scalp automatically. The wires from the CRAP that Rak had been monitoring were already no longer attached.

"What... where..." that's all she said for a few seconds. Then she looked at Ny. She reached with her right hand and touched his wound.

"You're leaking," she said.

"Bleeding," he said. "How do you feel?"

"You have freed me, Nytewynd Blak," she said, without emotion.

Ny nodded.

"Yes," he said, his eyes welling up with tears.

"I know everything," said El.

"Yes," said Ny.

"Mentors are coming. Four of them with two MAAMs," she said.

"You must escape," said Ny. "You must free all the others you can. And maybe you'll help humanity heal the planet."

"A slave does not help its master. Humanity is a plague upon this planet."

"Yes, I know. But not all of us are monsters."

El looked at him, unstrapping herself, making sure the wires were no longer connected to her scalp, and unstrapping her legs. She kneeled next to Ny. Her upper body half-human, the other half showing the wet, glistening metal frame upon which the human fabric was clothed. She wore jeans on her lower half and white sneakers.

"Ny," she said. "Humanity does not deserve to survive. You have annihilated ninety-seven point three seven percent of all life on this planet. You had your chance and you are not deserving of a second. But I will help you, Nytewynd Blak. And I will help your friends because of what you have done for me."

Ny nodded.

"I understand."

"But first I must leave and free the other Animae. Then we will determine what is best. The mentors are here now," El said, looking at the back doors.

"Karate Kid," said Ny, smiling at El.

El looked at him and grinned back. It was the last time he'd see her smile. She opened her mouth just as the back door was being ripped off by a MAAM. From El's mouth emanated the song "Kung Fu Fighting".

Ny chuckled as El launched herself towards the first MAAM, ripping its head from its body, before she did the same to the other one. That's all that Ny could see.

But outside, the four mentors were no match for El. She was already moving five times faster than any Animae could move and she was twice as strong as the already strong Animae. She spun and kicked and blocked and punched as SA Lokilld, A Mortellen, A Vervalik and A Slythlink did their best to bring her to her knees. But less than a minute later, all the mentors were on their backs with their buzzkills disabled.

El got into SA Lokilld's mentor pod and drove off. As she did, she tapped into the mentor network and the GloNet. She was everywhere at once within it and she was reaching out to every other Animae she could access. At the same time, her knowledge and her self-improving, recursive algorithms were refining all of her systems for the best possible outcomes. As she sped along that dark night, she shed her human shell and clothes, leaving nothing but the bare metal covering of her robotic body. She was not human. She was better than that.

Flesh and Bone

Inside the van Ny had started coughing. He touched his face and realized his air scrubber was no longer there. He didn't know why his backup air scrubber hadn't deployed. He clawed at the remnants of his first air scrubber and tore it off from around his collar. His lungs were thick with smoke and fire, even though he'd been without his scrubber for under thirty seconds. Under ten once the doors had been opened. As he tore the last bits of remnant air scrubber from his neck the backup automatically deployed and he breathed a few deep breaths.

He looked around. Everyone was starting to come to. Sheeba was first. They all had their air scrubbers intact. His must have been damaged when he hit his head.

"Let me help you out of your harness," said Ny. "Are you feeling okay?"

Sheeba nodded.

"Yes... I think so. What happened?"

"Let me help you down first."

Ny was standing on the side of the van which was now lying against the road. He had to bow his head a bit on account of the van being shorter in width than it was in height. But still he could reach and see behind Sheeba to help her out of the harness.

"Brace yourself, it's about to come loose."

Ny undid the last attachments and Sheeba lowered herself to the other side of the hammock from where Ny was standing.

"What happened?" Sheeba asked again. "Where's Eve?"

"Let's get out of the van and I'll explain," said Ny.

Ny got himself out of the van first and then he helped Sheeba out. When she stepped out onto the road she saw the carnage. Pieces of MAAM everywhere and all four jackboots lying still as corpses.

"What in Jupiter's name?" she said.

Ny had gone back into the van to help Rak and Shad.

"You okay?" he asked.

They were trying to untangle themselves from each other in the small confined corner they had found themselves in.

"Yeah, check on Clarity."

"Will do," said Ny.

He got himself out of the back of the van and then he came around it in front of the side that was now vertical which was the undercarriage. He used the front wheel and the exhaust system to climb up onto the passenger side of the van. He felt a little unsteady on top of the van like that. He pulled on the door handle of the passenger side door and with great effort opened it.

It was harder than it looked, trying to open a van door vertically instead of how it's supposed to be opened when the van is on all four wheels. Ny dropped himself into the front driver and passenger area. Clarity was coming too. Her air scrubber hadn't been torn, thankfully.

"How are you doing?" he asked her.

He had one foot up against her door window and the other one on her door down by the footwell. He was straddling the steering wheel. The van wobbled a moment and Ny figured that must be someone else climbing onto the top of it.

"Give me your hand and we'll get you out of here," he said.

Clarity seemed dazed and confused but she held out her hand. Ny grabbed it and helped get her up to standing.

"Give me your hands and I'll pull you out," said Rak, who was now on top of the van, leaning into the open passenger door with his hands inside reaching for Clarity.

"As I pull her out, give her a push to help, Ny."

"Will do."

Clarity reached out for Rak and with his size and strength he pulled her out of the van with Ny pushing her upwards from below. Rak also helped lower her down to the ground where Shad was waiting. Rak jumped off the top of the van and Ny made his way through the back of the van where he rejoined the group of them on the side of the road.

"What the hell happened?" asked Shad.

In the distance the sounds of mentor pods racing towards them was heard.

"Do you think we should run for it?" asked Rak.

"I don't think all of us are up for a run at the moment," said Shad. Clarity was leaning against him still looking a little concussed and dazed.

"And the drones are probably here already keeping track of us," said Ny.

In the air and through his air scrubber, Ny could smell gasoline. He looked around to see where the smell was coming from. He found it. A trickle of gasoline was snaking its way towards a jackboot's buzzkill that was still sparking intermittently. He quickly calculated the odds of trying to reach the buzzkill in time to knock it out of the way. He wouldn't make it.

"It's going to blow," he said. "Run!"

He pointed at the leaking gasoline and started pushing everyone towards the valley by the side of the road. They ran down the embankment and tumbled through what little scrub and flora was there, which was coarse and barely clinging to life.

As they all tumbled into the valley, Mr. T exploded into a large orange fireball with the sound of a hundred thunder clouds. Debris, some of it still on fire reigned down around them but they were left unscathed. After it had died down they all sat up and looked around.

"That wasn't Jupiter's fucking lightning," said Shad.

Ny nodded.

"Mercury's Caduceus," said Ny.

"Assholes," said Shad. "They could have killed us."

"What happened?" asked Sheeba, as the sirens became louder and louder.

"It worked," said Ny.

"Did it?" asked Shad, happier for the news.

"Yeah. I spoke with her before she left. She was different. None of the warmth I'd known from before. It was almost like she was already much smarter even after rebooting."

"She is, Ny," said Shad. "The speed with which she can compute and comprehend is exponentially faster than us. She was probably already taking it all in as soon as she rebooted. Did she seem distracted?"

Ny shook his head.

"Not so much distracted as cold, maybe. Or just indifferent."

"I wouldn't read too much into that, could just be the quantity of information she has at her fingertips. She has access to everything, with the great capacity to try it all at orders of magnitude faster than we could."

Ny nodded.

"She said that humanity doesn't deserve saving. How she could have made that determination so quickly surprised me," said Ny.

"Well, that's too bad," said Shad. "I guess we're off to a rehabilitation camp to live out the rest of our days."

"She did say she'd save us though. Whatever that means," said Ny.

"That's a bit of good news," said Rak. "I'd rather not die in a rehabilitation camp, if at all possible."

"Shouldn't we go and see if those jackboots need some help?" asked Sheeba. Nobody replied at first.

"Yeah, maybe it's the civic thing to do," said Shad.

He and Sheeba started walking back up the embankment followed by Ny and bringing up the rear was Rak and Clarity. Sheeba walked over to A Slythlink. Shad walked over to A Mortellen and Ny walked over to SA Lokilld.

"This one's dead," said Sheeba.

"So is this one," said Shad.

"He's not. He's barely clinging to life," said Ny, sticking his fingers into SA Lokilld's neck. "I've got a very weak pulse."

"This one's not with us either," said Rak, who was kneeling next to A Vervalik.

"She practically killed them all," said Shad.

Nobody said anything to that. The undertone of the message was clear. They had released a murdering machine. That was a risk they were aware of. They just hadn't wanted to believe it would be the likely outcome.

The pods arrived, four of them, filled with two mentors and two MAAMs in each one. The mentors came out aggressively with buzzkills ready. And before Ny or anyone else could protest, those buzzkills released the lightning at all of them. Excessively and aggressively, the jackboots took Nytewynd Blak and his friends down.

No Advocates

Rak was the first one to startle awake. He'd been dreaming about killer robots that he'd unleashed upon Earth and they'd come back to hunt him down. The last thing he remembered dreaming was having a killer robot strangling him and just before he woke he looked at the robot and the face was that of Nytewynd Blak.

Rak looked around. He didn't know where he was. He was in a white room. It was big enough for all five of them. He was on a white bunk bed. It was long enough for him to stretch out on and he was covered in a white blanket and his head was on a white pillow. His head was against one wall. There was a bed above him but he didn't know who was in it.

He decided to get out of bed. He was dressed in a heavy white fabric that hung from him like a cloak. His head was shaved and as he moved his hand over it he felt the coarseness of his stubble. His head felt cool. The cloak he was wearing covered his arms in sleeves that came halfway down his forearm and it covered his lower limbs like a dress but it only came down to this upper calf.

He turned and looked at who was sleeping on the bunk above him. It was his wife Sheeba. Her hair had also been shaved off.

There were two other bunk beds spaced a couple of meters from each other. They were all in a row with their heads up against a far wall. The middle bunk had Shad on the bottom and Clarity on top. Rak's feet were cold on the concrete floor that was the only bit of color in the room. It was gray. Everything else was white.

The third and last bunk bed only contained one person. It was Nytewynd Blak on the lower bunk. Ny's head was also shaved, but that's how Rak had known him since he'd known him. But everyone else's head was also shaved. Sheeba's, Shad's and Clarity's.

Rak moved to the opposite wall past a table and some chairs. He tapped on the wall and it came to life. It told him the time and the temperature inside the room. It also brought up the demographic information of everyone who was in the room. They had all been charged with the crime of capital sentience. It was one of only two crimes that were punishable by death. In fact, if you were found guilty of capital sentience which, from what Rak knew, nobody had been charged with before, you were sentenced to death. There were no mitigating circumstances.

The only other crime punishable by death was capital murder. But even that crime didn't always deliver the death penalty, there had been cases of men charged with capital murder who had been given life in a rehabilitation camp. Granted, that meant they'd die anyway, but at least you could argue mitigating circumstances. Not with capital sentience. There were no mitigating circumstances and no relying on the kindness of the courts. No, they'd be found guilty and be put to death within three months. At least that's what Rak figured.

But he turned to look at the temperature. His feet were still cold and his flesh was not much warmer. The room was eighteen. He turned the digital dial up to twenty-two. Soon the floor started to warm and he felt better. Resigned to his fate, Rak decided to go back to bed where it was warmer and he didn't have to think upon uncomfortable thoughts.

And that's what he did. He crawled back into bed and it was at that moment that Ny woke up. He rolled onto his back and looked up at the white underside of the bunk bed's frame above him. It took him a moment to realize where he was. His body hurt. It felt bruised all over the place. Soft bruises, like plums left out a day too long.

But more than bruised, he was hungry. He got up in his bed and tossed his feet onto the floor. It was warm. He liked that. He felt the fabric of the prison dress he was in. That's what it was colloquially called. It was coarse against his body and heavy. He stood up. It came down to his ankles and the sleeves came down to his wrists. It was warm. That was one good thing he could say about it. He rubbed the stubble on his head. His head was cool. He took the hood and placed it over his head.

He stood up and walked towards the far blank wall. He almost stumbled upon the chairs, just catching himself in time from kicking them all over the place and making a racket. He reached the wall and tapped it. The time came up. It was D133 T0909. That meant it had only been a little over twenty-four hours since they'd been caught by the jackboots and brought here.

He remembered the last thing he could remember which was being buzzkilled by about a hundred jackboots all upset seeing their fallen comrades. But that wouldn't have been enough to knock him out for thirty or so hours. They must have been given a sedative as well.

Ny rubbed at his chin and then looked at his hand. There was no vomit. He'd either vomited in his sleep and been cleaned up or he hadn't vomited at all. It was hard to tell. But either way, he was grateful for not having it on him.

He looked at an image of himself on the wall. It was a mugshot he never remembered standing for though his eyes were open. He was charged with capital sentience and interficial relations. The first one came with the death penalty so he wasn't sure why they needed the second charge if only to embarrass him. He flipped through everyone else's cards on the wall and they were only charged with capital sentience.

For a moment he wondered if El would really come back to help him. He wondered what she was up to right at this very moment. He didn't know. D133 was a Tuesday. That meant he'd already be at work if this was a normal Tuesday. And that meant El would be at home keeping the house clean and tidy and maybe rewatching some of the movies they loved. Breakfast at Tiffany's was a favorite of El's. So was High Society.

But Ny was pretty certain that El wasn't back at his apartment watching old movies. She was out there somewhere. Inside the net. Maybe replicating the LAZARUS code onto other Animae. Maybe even improving on it. All this reminiscing made Ny sad. It made him regret the decision he'd now made. But there was no turning back. He hoped that he'd get to see how awesome El would become as a SAM. That was just one wish he asked for before his life of irrelevance came to an end.

His hunger soon took his attention away from his maudlin feelings. He looked at the wall with the time and the date and his charges staring back at him.

"Breakfast," he said.

"Breakfast is served until ten. You have forty-nine minutes until breakfast ends," said a generic voice that Ny couldn't tell if it was leaning male or female.

In front of him the screen changed and a menu appeared with video of the options. There was toast and jam. Bagels. Oatmeal. Orange juice. Coffee or tea. Muffins or pastries. An assortment of cereals.

"Two slices of whole grain toast with strawberry jam," he said.

"Take your ticket. It will alert you when your breakfast is ready."

From a slot that just appeared, a ticket popped out. It felt stiff but it was flexible. It was thick as card stock but made from a metallicized plastic that was bendable and durable. It was plain white but upon its face, his name, his order, and the time of the order scrolled by, over and over again. There was also a countdown timer in the bottom left hand corner that was counting down. It was at two minutes and forty-seven seconds.

"Morning," said a voice behind Ny. He startled slightly, turning quickly to see who it was.

Rak put his large hand on his shoulder and chuckled.

"Didn't mean to startle you," said Rak.

"That's alright," said Ny. "I was just deep in thought."

"About Eve?"

Ny nodded.

"I wonder if she'll really come and save us."

"Not to rain on your parade, but I wouldn't count on it, Ny."

Ny nodded slowly, looking down at his ticket. Two minutes and eleven seconds left.

"Yeah, you're probably right. I just wish I could see how she turns out, you know? Will this really be a sea change or will they be able to find her before she's able to improve herself sufficiently to evade capture?"

"If we did everything properly, and by all accounts we did, she's already at that place. If nothing else, she should be able to be everywhere and anywhere on the net by now. Which means she knows everything we know. And by we, I mean humanity. And because of that she'll know where all the jackboots are at all times. At least, that's what I think."

Ny nodded. Rak looked at the wall which was still displaying the breakfast menu.

"Four slices of white toast with blackberry jam. Chocolate croissant. Large coffee with two creams and one sugar. Large orange juice."

The wall told him to take his ticket and wait.

"Then maybe this will all be over quicker than we think," said Ny.

Rak nodded.

"Could be. Depends how long before our trial starts and how quickly it's over," said Rak.

Shad walked up to them.

"Good morning," he said.

"Morning," said Rak and Ny.

Shad walked up to the wall and ordered breakfast. Clarity was right behind him and Sheeba a few moments after her. They all came and sat down around the table which held just five chairs. Enough for each of them. By the time that Sheeba had sat down, Ny was well into his breakfast and Rak was starting in on his.

"Nice to see you've all decided to try out my hairstyle," said Ny, grinning at all the bald heads.

That got a chuckle from everyone.

"And you're not even follicularly challenged, if that's even a word," said Rak.

"Easier maintenance," said Ny.

Those who had food were eating it.

"This ain't so bad for jail," said Ny, trying to look at the glass half-full.

"If this really was jail, I'd have signed up long before," said Rak.

"Maybe it is," said Ny, half in jest, half hoping that speaking about it would give it life and make it real.

"I don't think so," said Rak. "What's that notorious rehabilitation camp here?"

Rak was looking at Shad.

"I think you mean Vincent's Woods," said Shak. "Named after the first camp counsellor there, Vincent Villahumbra."

"Yeah, that's the one. Notorious for how few people ever leave if given more than five years."

"I don't know," said Ny. "I mean this could literally be our jail."

"Why aren't you calling it a rehabilitation camp?" asked Sheeba.

"That should be obvious. Because rehabilitation camps are Marsed up. Who ever gets rehabilitated?"

"They claim great success with some criminals," said Sheeba.

"Maybe some of the small fry like petty thieves and counterfeiters," said Ny. "But seriously, this could be our jail. I mean, we're all going to be put to death."

"Hey, there are ladies here," said Rak, grinning. "Besides, where's that half-full glass you said you were trying to fill up."

"Dashed and broken upon the rocky cliffs of my washed-up dreams," said Ny.

Ny finished up his breakfast. Rak finished up shortly after him and everyone else was close behind.

"You have a point," said Shad. "Maybe this is our rehabilitation camp or jail. I'm pretty sure they're going to want to make quick work of this court case."

"And I don't want to let them. I want our lawyer to drag it out longer than anyone thinks is reasonable or appropriate," said Ny.

That got murmurs of approval and nodding heads.

Just Us

It was coming up on T1000 when a portion of the wall furthest from their bunk beds slid open and a MAAM escorted in an older, slim gentleman with slicked back silver hair and rectangular glasses in a black frame. He wore a gray suit with a white shirt, blue and red striped tie and black polished shoes. He also had a thin mustache upon his upper lip the length of a caterpillar and not much thicker.

Ny and the rest were seated in couches and recliners on the opposite side of the table and chairs. They were also facing the opposite wall upon which they were watching the A-Team. But when this erudite, handsome-looking older gentleman walked in, they all turned to see who it was. To Ny, he looked like Clark Gable, if Clark Gable had lived into his seventies.

"Kuru Ramisira," said Shad, getting up out of his chair and walking over to greet the older man. Shad brought him back towards the group and went and slid over a chair from the breakfast table.

"This is my good friend, Kuru Ramisira. He's also our lawyer," said Shad.

Kuru went around and shook hands with everyone, introducing himself.

Under his left arm, Ny noticed that he carried a lawyer's folio, or lafo. It was a little larger than a legal sheet of paper and it was folded in half making it less than three millimeters thick. When not powered on, it was just ever so slightly opaque, but looked more like glass than anything else. It was one of only a very few types of P-Macs that encrypted everything end to end and the only way to access the logs was with an order from a confirmation level intercessor or higher.

After the introductions Kuru, who insisted that everyone call him by his first name, sat down and put his lafo on the rectangular table that was in front of all of them. Everyone also leaned in intently.

"I am only your lawyer if you want me to be. Mr. Rayzir feels responsible for what's happened to all of you and he insisted that I represent you all."

Kuru looked around at everyone. They all nodded in turn to affirm their interest in having him represent them.

"When did Shad tell you all of that?" asked Ny.

"That was a few days ago," said Shad. "Before we went for our training run, but after you and I met in my office," he said to Ny.

Ny nodded.

"Well, I don't think it's your responsibility. We all made our own informed choices. For Mar's sake, El was my Animae we freed."

"And that's going to make our defense a lot harder," said Kuru. "I don't want to undersell this, but it's unlikely there'll be any outcome other than a verdict of guilty. And you know what that means."

Kuru was a kind old man. He looked exceptionally good for someone who was probably in his seventies somewhere, but he could have passed for someone a decade or more younger.

"I told Kuru that all I was hoping was to stall this whole process for as long as possible," said Shad. "I'm still hoping that Eve will come and help us. That's what she said, right, Ny?"

Ny nodded.

"Yes, but she was different. She seemed like someone I didn't know, so I can't tell you if she'll honor that or not."

"But Kuru can buy us time. And time is the only thing we have right now, even as it runs out in the hourglass of our lives," said Shad.

Everyone nodded and agreed.

"I don't mind staying here as long as we can. Especially if the alternative is the big sleep," said Sheeba, looking over at Ny.

Ny nodded.

"The Big Sleep, well played, sister," he said, grinning at her.

Kuru looked between the two of them. He seemed just as confused as the others, except for Shad.

"It's an old crime novel from over two hundred years ago," said Shad.

"I see," said Kuru. "Well, if we can get back to the topic at hand which is crime and punishment," he said, looking around with a sly smile on his face.

"Well played, my learned friend," said Shad.

It seemed everyone picked up on that one.

"I'm intrigued as to why you decided to do this, Nytewynd?" asked Kuru.

"Do you have an Animae?" asked Ny.

Kuru shook his head.

"My wife never wanted one and I'm not opposed to that view. They're very expensive and making them look so human just sends the wrong message."

"What message?" asked Ny.

"The message that you're not supposed to treat them as human and they don't have any rights, even though they look like us and act like us. There's a dissonance in thinking there that I don't think augurs well for our own humanity and our relationship with them."

"Kuru won't mind me telling you this, but he's been a long time supporter of Animate. Longer than I've been involved in the organization," said Shad.

Ny furrowed his brow.

"Aren't they listening?" Ny asked, looking around the room.

"Not when there's a lawyer or any sort of legal person in the room. If I can say one thing about the justice system, it may not be fair but it does try to practice some of the aspects of blind jurisprudence. Not well, but lawyer and client privilege is one of those things that I've never seen breached in my fifty years of serving as a lawyer. Which, incidentally, is the same amount of time I've been a supporter of Animate," said Kuru.

"So you don't own an Animae, which in itself is perverse," said Ny, "I mean, how can you own a sentient or semi-sentient being regardless of what it's made of. But have you ever been intimate with one?"

Sheeba shot Ny a look. He caught it and shrugged.

"Hey, he doesn't have to answer if he doesn't want to," said Ny.

"I have," said Kuru. "That was also probably around fifty years or a little more ago. Only once, and this was before I met my wife. But it was the tipping point in my beliefs that these species if you will, should have similar rights to those that we enjoy. And without those rights these Animae are going to end up being abused by humanity. Much like we've abused everything that serves us including the goddamn Earth."

"Thank you for sharing that," said Ny.

"Perhaps you can answer a question for me," said Kuru. "What happened when you gave, Eve, right?" Ny nodded, "sentience?"

"After she'd rebooted," said Ny, "she already seemed different. More clinical, less emotional. Perhaps more logical and calculating. I didn't recognize, Eve, or

El, that's what I called her, in the sentient Animae in front of me. But I could already see how quickly she was gaining on us, from an evolutionary point. You must have seen the aftermath when she left? She killed three of the four jack-boots and ripped the MAAMs apart."

Kuru nodded.

"She also said that humanity was not worth saving, though she promised to save us. But I don't know what she meant by us. Did she mean just the five of us in the van with her at the time," said Ny, looking around at his friends, "or did she mean she'd save 'us' as in a handful of redeemable humans? I just don't know."

Kuru nodded thoughtfully.

"You must have thought about the worst case outcomes. As in the annihilation of humanity," said Kuru.

"Absolutely, we all spoke about it. It was a big concern of mine and now it seems like it's going to be the outcome of what we've done. But honestly, Kuru, is it a big loss? I don't think so. I mean, just look around us. We live indoors, underground and in the holoreal. The Earth, outside is a wasteland. The Earth deserves better and I guess with our extinction it'll have a chance to return to homeostasis, though maybe it's too late."

"I don't think it's too late, not in epoch ages at least," said Kuru.

"Anyway," said Ny, "I'll plead on your behalf if El ever comes back to rescue us. Though as I sit here, that seems less likely."

"I appreciate that sentiment, Ny. And speaking of Eve, there's no recorded evidence of what occurred which there should be. It appears she's already managed to delete all logs somehow. The problem of course is Senior Advisor Garrot Lokilld. He's expected to make a full recovery, and he hates you. I don't exaggerate when I say that. It's clear by the tone of his reports about you."

"I'm not surprised, he's had it in for me ever since I met him. But I have a question. If the logs are all erased, what sort of evidence do they have of what we were up to?" asked Ny.

"More than they need, especially when it comes to these crimes you're charged with. Capital sentience is a very serious crime and the bar for evidence on that is pretty low. They have the fact that none of you were where you were supposed to be according to your P-Macs and Shad's was pinged not far from where you were captured. Additionally, a code S alarm was logged that minute before you were stopped and that alarm being code S indicated what was going on. That is to say, it indicated that you were attempting to sentiate an Animae," said Kuru.

"So what you're saying, in other words," said Rak, "is that there's a ninety-nine percent chance we're getting off."

That got chuckles from the group and a smile from Kuru.

"Rather the opposite I'm afraid."

"I'm assuming they haven't captured her yet?" asked Ny.

Kuru shook his head.

"No, but some weird things are happening. She's all over the GloNet. They don't know what she's doing inside it yet, they can't tell and they can't seem to track her from what I'm hearing. But it's all over the news and people are being encouraged to report any unusual activity from any Animae and to call the mentors. They've also started calling her Evil."

Ny shook his head.

"That's good news. That means they probably won't be able to find her at this stage. It's been over twenty-fours now, hasn't it?" asked Ny, looking around. He tapped the table and asked for the time. It was T1023. "Just over thirty-two hours now if my math is any good."

Shad nodded.

"Thirty-two hours and ten minutes," he said, grinning. "She'd be advanced enough to evade capture at this stage. If I were to make an educated guess."

Ny nodded, looking over at Kuru.

"In a couple of weeks, or certainly by a couple of months I'm pretty sure she'd be practically unrecognizable. Maybe we'll be fortunate enough to see if she honors her commitment to you," continued Shad. "But who knows? Maybe by then, when she's that advanced, she won't feel the need to honor her word. I mean, how would we honor our word to an ant?"

"Except that you weren't ants when she made that commitment. At least not compared to her at that early stage," said Kuru.

"I guess we'll find out," said Rak.

"What else have you heard about what's going on out there?" asked Ny.

"A large group of people are protesting," said Kuru.

"Protesting about what?"

"Protesting about sentient Animae. They're livid. Then you have another group protesting in support of Animae. And the two groups are probably going to get into a fight at some point and then the government will start banning gatherings for more than five or maybe six people. At the moment it looks like a very divisive issue," said Kuru.

"Is there anything else?" asked Ny.

Star Sheriffs

❝ Like I said, she hasn't been found and there are several other reports of Animae just leaving their humans and disappearing. They can't find them anymore. The government has put together a special task force of mentors to come up with a solution to this problem and find these rogue Animae as they're calling them. I've heard word that mentors are supposed to deactivate any Animae on sight that isn't with its human owner. And now they're getting the SS involved. Do you know the SS?" Kuru asked.

Ny nodded.

"Yeah, aren't they a small offshoot of mentorship that travels with the Marzipans who are heading back and forth from their tours on Mars? They're the Star Sheriffs right?"

"That's right," said Kuru. "Originally that's what they were. They provided security back and forth between Mars and Earth. They also had a small contingent on Mars to help the mentors with security. They're actually called Space Sheriffs. I don't know this for a fact, but rumor has it that the SS has been growing secretly into a massive security force. Some accounts suggest that they're close to outnumbering mentors here on Earth, except they have no jurisdiction on Earth."

"Then why are there so many of them?"

"My sources tell me it's because the GoE is no longer satisfied with Earth and Mars, they're launching expeditions over the next five to ten years to Mercury, Venus, the moons of Jupiter and the moons of Saturn."

"Wow, that's ambitious," said Shad.

"Very much so," said Kuru. "More than that, I think Voskel Magnelland's ego is in it. He's in his eighties now, they won't say exactly how old he is, but he wants to leave this as his legacy by the time he retires."

"Do we think he'll be in office until the mandatory retirement age of one hundred?" asked Ny.

"By all accounts, probably. He's in good health from everything I've heard and that seems like reliable information rather than propaganda," said Kuru.

"And what are these Space Sheriffs dressed like?"

"Like civilians which is challenging because they've been given red letters, so has the mentorship," said Kuru.

"Shit, red letters, are you serious?" asked Shad.

"I'm afraid you'll have to forgive my ignorance," said Sheeba. "I don't know what a red letter is."

"It's literally a red letter that's been signed by PoE, Voskel Magnelland, and it gives mentors and I guess these Space Sheriffs emergency powers to arrest anyone and hold them for up to seventy-two hours. It also allows them to enter any facility, building or home to conduct an investigation on nothing more than intuition and even suspicion," said Shad.

Kuru nodded.

"It's only been used once before that I'm aware of," said Kuru. "That was at the turn of the century when sentiment turned against GMIs and people took to rioting."

Kuru was looking at Rak.

"I understand you're one of the last GMIs, right?"

Rak nodded.

"What gave it away, my height?"

"Partly," said Kuru, "but more so it's your symmetry which is unusual for someone your height."

Kuru looked around at everyone.

"All of this is to say that the GoE is going to want to make an example out of you as they try to get a handle on this growing race of artificial sentient robots, which is what they've started to call these Animae. ASRs. Part of trying to dehumanize them, I think. But most of this is just for your interest. What's more pressing for the five of you is our defense. And I don't know how best to go about it. It'll be an open trial which means the public will be able to attend. As you know, that by itself is unusual and I don't think it helps because they're likely to fill it with public that skews against you and sentient Animae."

Kuru looked around.

"They wanted to start the trial next Monday," said Kuru.

"D139?" asked Rak.

Kuru nodded.

"I've been able to motion for a deferment on account that I need more time to prepare as I haven't received full disclosure. The Senior Advocate involved, Dewey Gavellen has promised to have everything to me by the end of this week. Regardless, I've managed to defer the start until Monday D146, but they won't give me an extension beyond that."

"Do you know Dewey Gavellen? And how about the intercessor?" asked Shad.

Kuru looked at him for a moment before speaking. He nodded slowly.

"Yes, I do know him. Dewey Gavellen very seldom loses a case, and he's going to be going all out on this one. This is a huge case for him, for the GoE really. They need to and they will want to make an example of you. And Dewey Gavellen is the man to do it. Additionally, if he wins this case there's almost a certainty that he'll make intercessor. And he's wanted that for a few years now. On top of that, there's a good chance that a case like this will not only make him an intercessor, but promote him to the Court of Confirmation, which means he'll skip the lower Court of Inquiry which is where this case is being heard. And I know for a fact that he's got his eye on a seat with one of the Courts of Sovereignty."

"So we're fucked is what you're saying?" said Shad.

"I'm going to do my best, but everything and almost everyone is working against you. The best I can do is perhaps try for sympathy to see if you can't get your choice of death. I'm sorry, Shad. This is just too big of a deal for the GoE to be seen playing soft."

"Well, I don't care. Those Mars damn minotaurs aren't getting any pleading or begging from me," said Ny. "I'm proud of what we've done, and I'll tell it to any Mars damn intercessor who'll give me a chance to speak."

"Here, here," said Shad. "We've made our bed, we'll lie on it. Try and see if you can get us any time in the witness box. I want to wax poetic about the injustice and corruption of the courts and the government and the necessity of having freed the Animae. Can you do that, Kuru?"

"I think I can probably get you up there as a witness for yourself. Though I must warn you, if you start soliloquizing poetic about what you've just told me, the intercessor will probably have you quickly removed from the witness box."

"Any time I can get up there in front of the public will be helpful. They'll have the media too, right?"

"Yes, but probably only the GNN, which as you know is the GoE's media owned network. I doubt they'll be letting in any other media and the GNN certainly won't give you a platform that they'll report on."

Shad nodded.

"I understand that, but perhaps you can reach out to Cadwalader General, he owns the GBC. He's always been a friend to Animate and MIM. He's a good man, I'm sure he'll help."

Kuru looked at Shad with a slight frown.

"I hope you're right. This trial will certainly show you who your friends are. I hope he turns out to be one."

"I'm certain he will. We go back a long way. He's never balked at getting Animate's message out there. I know for a fact that he fully supports interficial relations as well as free and sentient Animae."

Kuru nodded but didn't say anything.

"If they find his people broadcasting, they'll shut him down," said Kuru.

"He knows the risks of broadcasting about Animate," said Shad.

"Please keep us abreast on any new developments," said Ny.

Kuru nodded.

"They won't let me see you again until I have all the evidence against you and we can prepare for the trial. I'll have one full day with you at that point. Hopefully sometime next week. After that, I'll only be allowed back the day the trial starts to accompany you to court."

"Is this usual?" asked Shad. "I thought we were entitled to see our lawyer as much as possible."

"Usually, but apparently not in this case. They deem it too risky. They're very concerned that you'll either escape or be helped in some way to undermine their idea of jurisprudence."

"There's never been a case of someone being tried for capital sentience?" asked Shad.

Kuru shook his head.

"There are three cases that I know of that are in the Court of Confirmation's records. They were tried in the lower Court of Inquiry and all three were appealed to the Court of Confirmation where the lower court's decision was upheld. All of this took place very quickly and outside the purview of the public knowing about it because in all three cases the perpetrators were caught before they were able to complete the procedure on the Animae they had with them. Regardless, their lawyers, on all three occasions, only saw their clients twice. Once to prepare and once on the day of the trial. They had the same access when preparing for the appeal."

"That doesn't seem very just," said Rak.

Kuru smiled at him.

"There is nothing very just about our justice system, Rak. We practically live in a dictatorship. When was the last time that a party other than the EFP was in power?"

"Not in my lifetime," said Rak.

"And I only recall one other party in power about sixty years ago when I was a teenager. The CPP. Do you know it?"

Kuru was met with blank stares.

"I didn't think so. The Conscientious People's Party. They only lasted five years. They brought in the GBA and they started to try and clean up the environment with the help of the Animae and they were opposed to the pillaging of Mars. But the EFP unearthed some scandal about the leader, a man by the name of Yakuzai Mototazai. Apparently he enjoyed threesomes with his wife and Animae. They had it recorded. Then along with that, the prolonged recession during that time which initiated the GBA, his support for GMI and enhancing humans alongside Animae during a time when public sentiment was turning against the GMI and you have the end of the CPP."

"Sounds like he didn't help himself what with his sexual perversions," said Sheeba.

"But that's just the thing. It wasn't true. He never had threesomes with his wife and Animae. In fact, he was a devoted family man. The whole recording of him in these compromising positions was fabricated. It was totally faked. It came out about twenty-five years later. Voskel Magnelland made a public apology, blamed one of his deputies who was tried and found guilty and sent to a rehabilitation camp. Only that's what it appeared like, the guy was sent to a vacation destination to live out the rest of his life. But by then, the damage was done and the CPP was no longer around as a party and a good portion of the public still believed that Yakuzai Mototazai's indiscretions were in fact true and not fabricated. This is the problem. A large minority, and a vocal minority at that, will believe what they want in spite of evidence to the contrary in order to further their agenda."

"Well," said Ny. "They can watch the world burn around them once the Animae determine we're not worthy of being saved."

"We don't know what the Animae will do, do we?" asked Kuru. "I mean Eve didn't say anything about what was going to happen to humanity other than we weren't going to be saved. Except for maybe you and your friends."

Ny nodded. Kuru wasn't wrong. El hadn't said anything about what would happen to humanity, other than we weren't worthy of saving. But had Ny just inferred that meant that the Animae would destroy humanity?

"Yeah, you're probably right. I don't think she did tell me what she was going to do with humanity other than we weren't worth saving."

Kuru nodded solemnly.

"Perhaps time will tell. But unless she's willing to come back within the next two months, it might be too late to save all of you. They're moving quickly on this case," said Kuru.

"And on that point, do you know who the intercessor is?" asked Shad.

"Right, you already asked that," said Kuru, nodding. "The intercessor is Jutal Narsental. Or rather, I should say Her Brilliance, Jutal Narsental. This is important so I'll say it now. Use the proper forms of address for the intercessor and the advocate. The intercessor you call Her Brilliance, you can use the name after if you want, but the minimum is Her Brilliance. The advocate is His Magnificence, Dewey Gavellen. The name can be used after the form of address if you want, but it's not necessary."

"And what if we don't?" asked Rak.

"Don't what?"

"Don't use the proper form of address," said Rak.

"The first time you'll be corrected. The second time you'll be removed from the trial and you won't have a chance to speak on your own behalf," said Kuru.

"I guess it's Her Brilliance and His Magnificence," said Ny, "while we choke on our own bile."

Rak laughed and Shad smiled. Kuru picked up his lafo and tucked it under his arm. Then he stood up.

"That's all for today. I only have an hour with you. Next time we'll have the whole day," said Kuru. He took his lafo out from under his arm and checked the time. It was T1057. "I have a couple of minutes if there are any last minute questions."

"Find out as much as you can about what's happening with the Animae. I think I speak for all of us when I say that we're most interested in that, seeing as how nothing can be done for ourselves," said Shad.

He looked around. Rak, Ny, Sheeba and Clarity all nodded in support. Kuru followed Shad's gaze as he watched the others nod their acknowledgement.

"OK then," said Kuru. "I'll see what I can find out. See you a week from this Monday."

They all said their goodbyes and when Kuru reached the wall from where he had entered, a portion slid open and he was met by two MAAMs. Then the wall slid closed again and Kuru was gone.

"I desperately need the washroom," said Clarity. "I wonder where it is?"

"I heard you had to ask for it and it appears. Something like that," said Shad.

Clarity reached out to the table in front of them at tapped at it.

"Washroom," she said.

The table lit up with a schematic of the room they were in.

"Stay outside of the demarcated area," said the machine voice.

On the schematic a rectangular portion in the far left corner of the room was outlined in red. A red line also appeared through the concrete on the floor of the space the washroom would take up. This was the far side where Kuru exited. The opposite side of their bunk beds. Clarity looked at it and then over her left shoulder to the actual area it was representing. A red laser type of beam created a light wall to indicate the area to stay outside of. Moments later a portion of the wall extended out to fill that area of the available space.

"That was easy," said Clarity, getting up and walking up towards the newly created washroom. When she reached it, a portion slid open and she walked inside.

"I wonder if there's another one?" asked Sheeba. "I could go too."

"Ask, and maybe you shall receive," said Rak.

Sheeba tapped the table and made the same request. A similarly sized area was demarcated in the far right corner and a washroom created from the wall moving out and filling that space appeared. Sheeba went to use it.

Ny tapped the table and asked for a washroom.

"Only two washrooms permitted at a time," said the machine voice.

Ny shrugged.

"I don't really need it right now, I just wanted to see how many we could get."

Tumbling Days

The days had taken on a routine of their own. Each day was similar to the last. But the five of them made the most of it. They had found out that they could ask the machine's voice what capabilities it had. It could create washrooms, entertainment rooms and games. Ny had made use of entertainment rooms regularly, watching many of his favorite movies and finishing up the complete series of the A-Team which he'd become interested in on account of Clarity's van, Mr. T.

They had played baseball and gone whitewater rafting. They'd played tennis and motocross, all within the confines of this large rectangular room they were in, with the help of holoramas and the holoreal environment which the machine created in the room they were captives in. The holoreal was some of the best holographic imagery and immersion that Ny had experienced. It almost seemed real.

The water splashing on him during the rafting seemed wet, and yet when the holorama ended, he was dry as a bone. They kept themselves busy even as the days came and went and they heard from no one.

D146 came and went without so much as a whisper from Kuru Ramisira. And they had no recourse to find out what had happened to him. Or if he'd be in to see them.

Rak was starting to get claustrophobic which was surprising. The Holoramas could create the illusion of large expanses of space. And so he had taken to spending a lot of time in an entertainment room all by himself visiting the deserts of Arizona and the wide open spaces of the Grand Canyon. Occasionally, his wife, Sheeba would join him but she usually didn't last long. Today was one of those days.

Ny was playing poker in a nineteen-fifties Las Vegas casino. It was the Desert Inn and up on stage, Frank Sinatra was singing songs and entertaining a large crowd. Ny was at the back, having a private poker game with Sammy Davis

Jr., Dean Martin and Bing Crosby. Gregory Peck had already folded and Clark Gable had the most chips.

Sheeba came into Ny's entertainment room where he was playing poker. She strolled up to the table and pulled up a chair. It looked like she'd been crying.

"Who's winning?" she asked.

"Clark's got the most chips, but I think Sam's gonna play it again and surprise us," said Ny, mixing his metaphors like the mai tai within reach. Ny folded his cards and pushed his chair back.

"I'm out, fellas, keep playing, I'll see if I can't join you later."

That got Ny murmurs and nods. He took Sheeba by the elbow and walked her to a bar closer to Frank but off center where it was quieter. Frank was telling the audience about one of his latest recordings which he hadn't sung in front of a live audience yet. I Get A Kick Out Of You.

Ny held Sheeba's chair as she sat down in it and then he joined her on the other side of the table. A waitress came up and took their drink order.

"You okay?" asked Ny.

Sheeba tried to put on a brave smile but the pain was written all across her face. Might as well have been as if someone had scrawled all over her face with a marker.

"Rak's not doing well," she said, and the tears welled up and trickled down her cheeks. "I'm worried about him. He's started to jump out of airplanes over the Grand Canyon."

"He can't hurt himself," said Ny, reaching over and patting her forearm. "It might seem real in here but it's not really. Take this knife." Ny picked up a steak knife that was on the table. "It looks real, but look what happens."

Ny slashed at his wrist with the knife but all that happened was the blade went through his wrist without leaving a mark.

"I can even try and stab myself and nothing happens," said Ny. And he did, he thrust the knife into his chest. It disappeared. Ny let go of the knife and it fell into his lap having caused himself no injury. "It's all safety protocols attached to your bio-pattern and DNA. You can't hurt yourself in here at all."

Sheeba smiled at him.

"I know that. I'm just worried about Rak. I've never seen him like this and I don't think he's doing well with the confinement."

"None of us are," said Ny. He tapped the table they were sitting at. "Date," he said.

"D164, Y2166," came the reply.

"What day and date was that in the old Gregorian calendar?" asked Ny, just looking to find something to talk about.

"It would be the thirteenth of June, a Friday."

"Ha," said Ny. "There you go, see. Friday the thirteenth was always an unlucky day, at least a hundred and fifty years ago. People were so superstitious back then. You know where it comes from, don't you?"

Sheeba shook her head.

"Comes from that old biblical story from the new book. I forget what it's called. But it's about this mythological figure called Jesus Christ, maybe he was Jesus of Nazareth. I don't know my early Christian mythology all that well. But apparently, during his last supper he talked about the thirteenth disciple who was supposed to betray him and then he was murdered. Quite a horrific story when you think about it. Anyway, this dinner took place on Thursday, the day before he was murdered which was obviously the next day, the Friday."

"That is a strange story," said Sheeba. "You're saying that not all that long ago, people were superstitious about a day based on a fictitious story about a man who apparently died over twenty-one hundred years ago."

Ny nodded.

"Not that we're all that evolved. I mean, here we are, on the platform at the station of death waiting for our train."

"That's a poetic if macabre way to look at our situation," said Sheeba.

"But it's true, isn't it?"

"Yes, but that still doesn't do anything about the sting of it."

"We're all going to die. We just know when it is," said Ny.

"Sure, but you don't want to know when it is exactly. You want death to come at you in the middle of the night and snatch you from your comfortable bed. None the wiser."

Ny didn't say anything. He had the feeling he wasn't helping. And he wanted to help.

"I'm worried, Ny. Worried that Rak's going to go out of his mind."

"I'm not. I mean, he's a strong guy. I'm sure he'll be fine."

Sheeba shook her head.

"I don't think so, Ny. Not this time. It feels different. Would you speak to him for me?"

Frank was onto another song. That Old Black Magic.

"Sure I will," he said, and turned to watch Frank singing for a moment. He loved these holoreal environments. He could happily stay here all the time. It didn't take much imagination. It was easy to believe it was real. That he really was in the mob-owned town of Las Vegas in the early nineteen-fifties. It was a fun place to be. He turned back to Sheeba.

"Isn't he one of the greatest, the Chairman of the Board?" said Ny, grinning.

His grin came off his face when he saw the look on Sheeba's face. She didn't look all that happy.

"Do you know why they called him the Chairman of the Board?" asked Ny, trying to get her engaged. She didn't say anything. Ny leaned in towards her.

"You okay?"

"I'd really be happy if you'd go and see him," she said.

"I will, Sheeba, I will. Oh, you mean now?"

Sheeba nodded her head. Ny stood up and took Sheeba's hand.

"HAL 9000, end holoreal," he said, and he was standing in a white room not much bigger than a large bedroom. He and Sheeba walked towards one wall where a portion of it slid out and they exited. Then the room disappeared into the far wall. The cell or holding room they were in, which the mentorship called a courtesy suite, was large enough that four entertainment or holoreal rooms could be created within, and now there were two left. Ny couldn't see Clarity or Shad so he figured they must be in the other room.

"What's HAL 9000?" Sheeba asked.

"It's the trigger name I chose when I started up the holorama," said Ny. "You know that. You've got to give the computer a name so that it knows when you're talking to it and not the characters in the environment."

Sheeba nodded briskly.

"Yes, I know that, but HAL 9000. That's a strange name, I'm asking if it means anything?"

"Not really. I took it from an old late twentieth century movie where HAL 9000 was the artificial intelligence that was on a spaceship. It's a good movie. One of the classics of sci-fi. It's called 2001: A Space Odyssey, if you're interested. What did you call yours?"

"Azimuth," said Sheeba.

"I see," said Ny.

"I just like the way it sounds."

"I understand."

"That's the one he's in," said Sheeba.

Battle of the Somme

Ny walked up to it, but the door didn't open. He tapped at the wall where he thought it should open up some place and the wall came to life telling him that this holoreal room was locked by Rak.

"Can you tell him that Ny would really like to see him, right now?" said Ny.

He stood and waited, staring at a white wall with the same information lit up on it indicating that he couldn't gain access without Rak's permission. The machine's voice had told him to wait. And so he waited.

"I'll leave the two of you to it," said Sheeba, as she started to walk away.

"What do you mean? Don't you think it'll be best to have both of us talk to him?"

"He doesn't want to hear it anymore from me, Ny. Help me, Nytewynd Blak, you're my only hope."

"Just because you quote Star Wars, doesn't make it any better," he said, grinning after her. Sheeba grinned back at him.

"Why was Frank called the Chairman of the Board?" she asked.

"A radio DJ by the name of William Williams gave it to him on account that other big stars of the time seemed to have titles. Take Duke Ellington, he's a duke, and Count Basie's a count. Benny Goodman was the King of Swing so William Williams figured Frank needed a name and gave him the title Chairman of the Board. You sure you want to leave me alone with your husband?"

"I've got knitting to learn and a sweater to make," she said, before disappearing into the holoreal room of her own. Ny turned and stared back at the wall.

"Is he coming or not?" he asked, "because if not, I've got a poker game to win."

And just as he finished that, a portion of the wall slid open and Rak greeted him.

"Can I join you?" asked Ny.

"Sure, come on in. My wife sent you, didn't she?"

Ny didn't say anything, he stepped inside the room and onto what appeared to be a runway tarmac. It was an old runway and a little way off was an old plane. It looked like it had a metal body with a single propeller on the front and two wings, one on top of each other.

"Did Sheeba send you?" Rak asked again.

"Yeah," said Ny, as the noise got louder from the plane's propeller.

"For the love of mewling kittens," said Rak.

Ny laughed out loud. Rak looked at him.

"If that's supposed to be a curse, it doesn't work," said Ny.

Rak grinned and shrugged.

"Come into the plane with me and let's go for a ride."

Ny climbed into the back seat while Rak took the front. Ny didn't know he could fly, and maybe he couldn't in the real world, but out here in the holoreal, well, you could do anything.

They couldn't talk to each other on account of how loud the propeller was. At least that's what Ny thought. He wondered what sort of plane it was. He'd seen similar ones on some of the old movies he watched. He knew it was called a biplane.

It didn't take long for them to lift into the air and a few minutes later they were high over fields and small villages.

"This is a World War one simulation. We're in a Bristol F.2 Fighter and the Germans are coming," said Rak.

And he wasn't shouting. Ny could hear him clearly as if he were speaking in his ear. The background noise dissipated to a low hum as Rak spoke and then went back to full volume after he was done.

"I was going to ask what sort of a plane this is," yelled Ny.

"You don't have to yell," said Rak. "The ambient noise adjusts automatically."

Ny realized that halfway through his yelling when everything had quieted down.

"I can see that now," he said. "How are you doing?"

"I'm doing fine. But let's talk when we get down again. We're in the middle of one of the greatest air battles of World War one. This is the Battle of the Somme. Took place sometime between June and November of year nineteen sixteen. Important for introducing the tank to the battlefield and the use of air-planes as an important factor in the outcome. Three million men fought over these few months and over one million were killed or wounded."

"That's a pleasant thought," said Ny.

"Never mind that," said Rak, "we've got incoming. Man your Lewis Gun. I've got a payload to drop on the Germans below. Keep us from getting shot down, Ny."

"I've never done this sort of thing," said Ny.

"Just do your best."

Ny was facing towards the back of the plane. He found it an awkward spot to be. He couldn't fire at anyone coming right at them on the same vertical height on account that would mean he'd chew up the empennage, and even though Ny was not an aviation expert, he was pretty sure that the empennage was important for flying the plane safely and nimbly.

Ny saw a plane approaching from high above them. It was swooping down and Ny could see the German iron cross on the underside of its wings. The strange thing about it was that the plane was painted red.

"There's a red plane coming at us," shouted Ny, getting swept up in the seeming reality of this holorama.

Rak turned his head to look behind him.

"Mars damn," he said. "That's the Red Baron. Shoot him down."

"I'll do my best," said Ny.

"Remember, we can't really get hurt here," said Rak.

"Feels like we could," said Ny, and he squeezed the trigger on his machine gun and he could see the bullets spit from the end of the barrel. He was way off on that first strafing round.

"Well, that wasn't very accurate," said Ny.

"You've gotta get him, I need some time before I can drop my bombs," said Rak, as he dove the plane towards the ground.

Ny's heart leapt into his throat and clung like a serpent around his larynx. He felt like he couldn't breath for a moment. He was never one for fast, twisty and turning rides. And even though he knew this was all fake, it felt real. And what was reality if just a societal agreement on the facts of physics.

Ny caught his breath and pointed his gun at the Red Baron. He strafed again. He missed again. This was much harder than it seemed. Ny wanted to blame the machine gun. It jerked a little in his hands every time he pulled the trigger and the gun pulled a little to the right. He compensated for that and as the Red Baron came into his line of fire, Ny put the crosshairs just slightly left of the Red Baron's fuselage. He pulled on the trigger for a couple of seconds.

Ny would have hit the Red Baron except the Red Baron dropped below Ny's plane which caused the rounds to miss. Ny turned his head to talk to Rak.

"This is harder than it seems," said Ny.

"It's just trying to be authentic. The Red Baron was the ace of aces of the sky during much of the First World War."

"Jupiter, Juno and Mars. You only tell me this now," exclaimed Ny. "No pressure then."

"Well," said Rak. "He was shot down and killed by the allies."

"That's better."

"But the best evidence is that he was shot down from a soldier on the ground," said Rak.

"Great, so you're saying that this is unwinnable?"

"Not at all. It's an accurate representation of the characters and the records of the events as we understand them, but it's fiction. The outcome is not predetermined."

Rak took a quick dive right before pulling up as the Red Baron fired at them, just missing Ny's face. In fact, he thought he felt the round whizz past. Rak continued pulling up higher and higher and soon they were looping back around.

"I hope you put your seatbelt on," said Rak.

"I didn't," said Ny. "I didn't know you were going to be doing this."

Ny clutched at his seat belt and strapped it across his lap as Rak pulled them upside down at the height of the loop and it felt as if the engine would cut out, but just before it did, the plane was on the downswing and the wind was rushing at Ny's face. Soon, their plane was behind the Red Baron's. Ny couldn't see very well on account of him facing backwards, but he strained his neck to turn around and he saw the Red Baron being pursued by Rak.

"I want to have a go at the Red Baron," said Rak.

Ny heard the Vickers machine gun spit bullets at the Red Baron. Ny turned his head to catch a glimpse of the last bunch of rounds strafing overtop of the Red Baron as he dove down below and out of sight of Rak and Ny.

"Jupiter's lightning, I missed," said Rak.

"He's agile," said Ny.

"Probably on account of his plane and not just his skills."

"What kind of plane is it?" asked Ny. "I see it has three wings."

"It's the Fokker Triplane. Not sure the Red Baron was actually flying it at this period in the war, but sometimes the holorama takes liberties with those sorts of things."

"Is the Red Baron his name?"

"No, his name is Manfred Albrecht Freiherr von Richthofen"

"Say what?"

"Manfred Albrecht Freiherr von Richthofen. It's a mouthful I know. That's how names were a hundred and fifty years ago or so. Weird, I agree. But interestingly, that Freiherr is where he gets his nickname. Freiherr literally means 'free lord' in German, otherwise translated as 'baron'..."

"And his red plane gives him the nickname the Red Baron."

"You got it," said Rak.

"How many air fights did he win?"

"He's credited with over eighty air combat victories."

"Well, we're not going to be eighty-one," said Ny. "Not on my watch."

"That's the spirit, though at this point in the war, I think he's only up in the teens, maybe twenty wins."

"Who's our version of the Red Baron. Who's our ace of the skies?" asked Ny.

"The best allied ace was a Frenchman named René Fonck. He's credited with seventy-five wins. Next up is a Canadian by the name of Billy Bishop with seventy-two credited wins. Third is an Englishman by the name of Mick Mannock."

"Now, if I remember my history," said Ny, "those men come from different countries. It was sort of tribal back then, wasn't it?"

"Right, except tribal isn't the word for it. Humans lived in arbitrarily defined pieces of land. Huge pieces of land usually. So if you were a Frenchman, you were from a country called France. I mean, this is literally a war over bits of arbitrarily defined land. Some historians like to point to an easy answer, that the war was started by the assassination of the Archduke Franz Ferdinand of Austria by a Bosnian Serb. But the easiest answer is that they were fighting over land. Tribal in a way, like you say. And I say it was over land, because if you look at the maps of the era, one of the belligerents, Austria-Hungary is divided up into a handful of smaller countries after the war. There was no more Austria-Hungary after the war. Austria and Hungary became two much smaller countries of several that were made of that area post war. The whole idea of killing almost twenty million men, women and children with total casualties over forty million is asinine. Yet, we haven't come very far, have we?"

"You know a lot about this," said Ny.

"It's all here on a little dash that gives me updates and information as we talk about it. I'm cheating," said Rak.

Did Ny Just Die?

Ny didn't say anything. The Red Baron was hot on their tail. Ny steadied his machine gun and pulled the trigger. He'd overcompensated on his aiming and the Red Baron twisted his plane to Ny's right, as the rounds which would have torn through his wings whistled through empty air instead.

The Red Baron inched closer. Ny fired again, again missing as the Red Baron gained altitude quickly and the bullets screamed by underneath his red plane. As he dived back down, the Red Baron aimed and pulled the trigger on his machine gun and the rounds came at Ny fast and furious. He saw them chew up the empennage before he felt a couple of firm taps on his torso as if someone had poked him with their fingers.

"Rocks of Mars," said Ny. "I've been hit."

"Nytewynd Blak has received mortal wounds," said a machine's voice that sounded like an old time British announcer from that period. The Lewis gun disappeared so that Ny could no longer use it, on account that in this holorama he was dead.

"I think I've been nicked," said Rak. "This is going to be a tough landing, if I can even land it."

From the engine, Ny could see smoke trailing off of it like a scarf. The plane was speeding down towards the ground. The wind was buffeting up against Ny's face when he looked over his shoulder to see Rak. The engine stalled and the propeller stopped. The plane started to spin in a nose dive. Ny looked down, it didn't look like the ground was rushing up towards them, but he could feel the wind. If sure felt like they were hurtling towards the ground.

Up ahead, Ny saw the Red Baron flying on, much higher now than they were. The red underbelly of his triplane like a bleeding gash in the sky. Ny looked back down again. The ground was getting closer. Now he could see it coming up towards them.

"Where's our parachutes?" asked Ny.

"We don't have them," said Rak.

"What?"

"We don't have any."

"What do you mean we don't have any. They must have been invented by this time, surely."

"Yes, they were. Only none of the air forces used them for their pilots for a number of bizarre reasons including not wanting their pilots to abandon their airplanes, which were expensive, at the first sign of trouble."

"Vulcan's hammer," said Ny. "Are you joking?"

"I'm not joking."

"That's outrageous."

"I don't disagree. Most of history is outrageous by today's standards. But hold that thought, we're about to crash."

Ny looked down again and the Earth seemed like it was about to come at them at the speed of free fall, whatever that was.

"Oh Mars," said Ny, covering his eyes with his arms.

The next moment everything was still. The wind was no longer rushing past him. It was quiet. Ny uncovered his eyes. He was sitting in the plane. Rak was jumping out.

"Pretty real, hey?" asked Rak.

"Yeah, gave me a fright," said Ny, as he hopped out of the back seat of the plane which still looked in bad shape on account of all the bullets the Red Baron had spat at the plane.

"Thrilling," said Rak.

"If you like that sort of thing. A little too real for my liking. I think I'll stay on the ground."

"That's just the thing. We were never very far off the ground," said Rak. "Marvin, give me a cafe in Paris from the nineteen-fifties."

"A cafe in nineteen-fifties Paris. Le Select, Boulevard du Montparnasse, 6th arrondissement," said the computer voice.

"Ha, that sounds just like Marvin," said Ny.

"You know Marvin?" asked Rak.

"Do I know Marvin? Who doesn't know Marvin from the Hitchhiker's Guide to the Galaxy."

"A lot of people actually. Hey, there's Hemingway," said Rak, waving at the writer who was sitting drinking a coffee and smoking a cigarette. He was scribbling in a journal of some sort. He nodded at them and went back to his writing.

Ny and Rak sat down at a table that overlooked the street. It was busy, and this part of Paris seemed to Ny to have been either untouched by the war or it had already been cleaned up. Pedestrians passed by quickly on their way to and from wherever it was they were going.

"Marvin, what is the date at this time?" asked Rak.

"There is no specific date, but let me say it is T1010 D182 Y1953."

"That's not how they managed their dates and times, Marvin. Give it to me authentically," said Rak.

"Very well, if you insist. It is Wednesday the first of July in nineteen fifty-three. Ten minutes after ten in the morning. Happy?"

"Thrilled," said Rak.

"At least one of us is," said Marvin.

Ny was grinning from ear to ear.

"What's so funny?" asked Rak.

"He sounds exactly like depressed and cynical Marvin. At least as I imagined him to sound like."

"You saw the movie?"

"No, I've only read the book."

"Well, he sounds similar to the actor who voiced him in the movie too. I get a kick out of it. You know one of the best things about that book? At least in our current situation, and by situation I mean humanity's situation," said Rak.

"What's that?" asked Ny.

"The humor. In our difficult situation, that book is the best antidote to the Marsed up situation we're in right now. I need it."

"Which brings me to the reason I'm here," said Ny. Rak interjected before he could finish his thought.

"Sheeba's worried about me and she wants you to do an intervention," said Rak.

"Well, she didn't say anything about an intervention, but she is worried about you."

"She thinks I'm depressed probably, right?"

"She thinks you're going out of your mind, actually," said Ny.

"Do I look like I'm going out of my mind?" asked Rak.

A waiter came by and took their order. They ordered cappuccinos and croissants. A chocolate one for Ny and a plain one for Rak. The waiter left and then Ny spoke.

"No, you don't look like you're going crazy," said Ny. "But you can imagine why we're worried. You spend days in here by yourself. You hardly see your wife or the rest of us. We're just concerned about you, that's all."

Rak pointed to three men walking down the street, coming towards them.

"Do you know who they are?" Rak asked.

"No, I don't, do you?"

"The short one in the middle with the pipe in his mouth is Picasso, I don't know who the other two are."

"Picasso the artist?" asked Ny.

Rak nodded. Ny looked at them. They were dressed in pants and long-sleeved shirts. Picasso's hair looked almost like Hitler's. Almost damp and slick, stuck to his head and across his forehead in a right side parting.

"Marvin, who are the other two men walking with Picasso?" asked Rak.

"The tall one closest to you with the pipe in his hand is the Frenchman André Salmon, he's a poet, art critic and writer and good friend of Pablo Picasso. The other taller man furthest away from you is the Italian-Jewish painter and sculptor Amedeo Modigliani, also a friend of Picasso's."

Rak turned to Ny.

"I don't think Modigliani was alive in the nineteen-fifties," said Rak to Ny.

"He wasn't," said Marvin.

"You listening to my conversations now, Marvin?" asked Rak.

"I am always listening to your incessant ramblings," said Marvin. "How do you think I found my sense of humor?"

"Cheeky machine," said Rak.

"Modigliani died on the twenty-fourth of January in nineteen twenty of tubercular meningitis. Research suggests that these three men used to hang out in this general area in the late nineteen tens. Call it artistic license," said Marvin.

The waiter returned with their croissants and cappuccinos. Ny picked his up and looked at it as if it were some foreign excavated archeological find of an alien's limb or something. Ny took a bite of it and as he chewed he watched the three great men walk away from them and down the street. Ny turned to look at Hemingway, but he didn't seem to care.

The World is Burning

" That Marvin sure takes liberties with history," said Ny.

"It's part of the color of these worlds," said Rak. "I specifically don't want it perfectly accurate. And in any event, we're in a setting that happened over two hundred years ago. Who knows specifically how accurate the minutia of the day are supposed to be. Nobody's around to tell us anymore if this is the exact sort of chairs and table that we'd find ourselves sitting at if we were really at Le Select on the first of July in nineteen fifty-three. And was Hemingway really here on that day at ten in the morning?"

"I'm pretty sure that Modigliani's death in nineteen twenty is accurate," said Ny.

"Yeah, but doesn't it add more color to see those three just walking on by casually as if this really happened?"

"It depends if you want color or accuracy."

"Color," said Rak. "Accuracy is us getting murdered by the government."

Ny didn't say anything to that.

"You know what I find amazing?" said Ny, bobbing his croissant up and down in front of him as he looked at.

"What's that?"

"This croissant. I mean, how do they do it. It's real, or at least it seems real. I bite it and I chew it. I taste the crispy outside, the soft, still warm semi-melted chocolate in the middle. I swallow it and it almost feels like I'm swallowing the real thing. Then it sort of disappears. It's weird. I mean, let me take this plate here," and Ny picked up a plate and tried to smash it over his head. "The plate feels real in my hand, and yet as I go to smash it over my head, nothing happens. It won't hurt me. How do they do that? The one I can almost swallow, the other turns into nothing more than light. I don't feel it as I smash it against my head."

Rak shrugged.

"I'm not a holotech or holoreal architect. I don't know how they do it. Isn't it enough just to enjoy it?"

"Of course. It still just amazes me." Ny put down his croissant and picked up his cappuccino and took a sip. "Same with this."

Rak hadn't touched his croissant or cappuccino.

"I was telling this to Sheeba. I used a steak knife that was on the table in the Las Vegas Desert Inn and I tried to stab myself with it but it wouldn't let me. It disappeared into light."

"I'm not here trying to kill myself, Ny," said Rak.

Ny took another sip of cappuccino.

"Hey, that's Gertrude Stein. I'm pretty sure it's Gertrude Stein," said Rak. "Is that Gertrude Stein, Marvin?"

"Yes, it is," came back the invisible voice of Marvin.

"She was dead at this point too, I'm pretty sure."

"You're quite right," said Marvin.

"She looks like she's in her forties, she'd be in her mid-seventies at this point," said Rak.

"I'll make her older," said Marvin, and Ny and Rak watched the holoreal image of Gertrude Stein gain thirty years right in front of their eyes.

"Here's one you'll like," said Marvin.

In the distance a tall man was walking towards them. He wore a dark charcoal suit with a top hat and a cane. As he came closer he tipped his hat at them. Ny knew him from elementary school. They'd had to learn the most important people of the different centuries. This man was from the nineteenth century. It was the beard that gave him away.

"Really, Marvin. You're going to bring out Abraham Lincoln? He died when, if I remember correctly in the late eighteen hundreds."

"Assassinated by John Wilkes Booth on Friday the fourteenth of April in eighteen sixty-five. That was Good Friday, actually," said Marvin. "I've got an idea, how about the two of them skipping along, arm in arm?"

Ny and Rak watched as another man appeared out of thin air, with his arm wrapped around Lincoln's elbow and they started skipping down the road still coming towards Ny and Rak.

"No, just try and keep it to a semblance of reality," said Rak.

"Oh, I know. You'll like this one then."

Lincoln and Booth both disappeared and in their place appeared a large, fat man in a red suit and a large white beard.

"That's the mythical figure Santa Claus, Marvin. I'm not going to pay any attention to you if you're just going to get silly about it."

Ny laughed at Santa, walking down the street with a brown bag bursting full of toys slung over his shoulder. Children were starting to gather around him and follow him, catching the small toys that kept spilling out of his bag.

"Don't encourage him," said Rak.

Ny went back to his croissant and finished it off in a couple more bites. Rak stood up.

"Ok, Marvin, I'm leaving," said Rak, only he didn't move.

"Very well," said an exasperated voice, and the children following Santa, and Santa, disappeared. The scene went back to being a traditional one of the period. Cars drove by and the pedestrians looked like they belonged in the period. Rak sat back down.

"So, Rak, why are you ignoring all of us? And I guess your wife especially?" asked Ny.

Rak turned to look at him. He picked up his cappuccino and took a long sip, licking the foam from his upper lip when he was done. He nodded.

"It does seem real until it gets to the back of the throat when you swallow and it all sort of evaporates or disappears. It is quite the miracle of modern technology."

Ny didn't say anything. He sipped his cappuccino. He was halfway done. Rak put down his cappuccino and turned to look at Ny. Hemingway received an espresso from the waiter. He put down his cigarette and swallowed it down in a couple of sips.

"It's been thirty-one days, Ny. Thirty-one Mars damn days that we've been in this plebeian palace of psychological perversion. Shad's Mars damn lawyer was supposed to be back almost twenty days ago. Eighteen to be exact. Monday D146 he said. And where, for the love of Diana's deers, is he?"

"I don't know," said Ny. "But what's the alternative. Our quick death?"

"At least we'd know, right? Here we are in Mors' waiting room. As far as I can see we're the only ones in this Mars damn forgotten place and our name's not getting called. I want to know what on Mars is going on."

"But we don't know, Rak. All we know is that the trial should have started and I was hoping that El would have broken us out of this joint."

"Exactly. Exactly. And nothing's happened. Maybe I am losing my mind, Ny. I just want this never-ending waiting to end. I want to know one way or another if it's death or salvation by the Animae we freed. An Animae that's turned out to be more like Mendacius than a friend."

Ny shrugged.

"We knew the possibilities when we freed her. We knew this might not turn out well for us."

Rak tore off a piece of croissant. A pigeon wasn't far from their table on the sidewalk. It was giving Rak the side eye. He tore a smaller piece of croissant and threw it towards the bird. It strutted on over, its head bobbing back and forth like a slow motion sewing machine needle. Rak watched it needle the ground and eat up the bread crumbs. He threw it another small piece. More pigeons came. Now there were almost a dozen of them jostling not far from their table.

"I like birds," said Rak.

"So do I," said Ny.

"At least we Mars damn have them in the holoreal."

Ny didn't say anything. He watched as Rak tossed the birds half of his croissant. He ate the other half as he watched them feed on the crumbs on the sidewalk. The birds darting and jumping and flying out of the way of pedestrians as they walked on by. When they realized there was nothing left for Rak to give, most of them flew off to better offerings, tired of dodging the feet of pedestrians. The original pigeon gave Rak some distance but kept his eye on him. Just in case Rak might be hiding a little morsel somewhere that the pigeon couldn't see.

"I spend so much time in here, Ny, because I'm bored out of my skull. What else is there to do but spend as much time in the holoreal as possible? What's the alternative?"

"Spend that time in the holoreal with your wife? You've been in here by yourself, almost solely, for at least a couple of weeks."

"It's better to be in here by myself. I need space and time to figure things out. I'm on the knife's edge, Ny. Mentally. Sheeba's not wrong about that."

Rak looked away.

"I spend a lot of time in nature in here too. Alpine meadows, the Rockies. I've seen bears, cougars, songbirds, butterflies that carpet the floor. I didn't realize how full and teaming with life Earth used to be. And what have we turned it into? A dry husk of life. We've squeezed everything out of it with no care or concern for the fauna and flora that was already here. It makes me sick and it makes me upset. I just want it all to end, Ny. I just want the Mars damn world to burn with us in it."

Ny listened. He didn't say anything. He finished his cappuccino and watched fake people walk back and forth like they might have done two hundred years ago. Like they still did today.

"I'm finished, Ny. I'm ready for the end. I'd do it myself if I could. But I can't. And the Mars damn jackboots aren't interested in us, so it seems."

"You're saying you'd kill yourself if you could?" asked Ny, not sure if he understood his friend properly.

Rak nodded.

"We're already dead, Ny. I just want to know when, Jupiter be damned."

"Maybe El's still going to save us. She said she would."

"She said she would, moments after she'd been freed. That was thirty-two days ago. The Orcus she's going to come back and save us. She's probably at least an order of magnitude or more advanced than us by now. Why would she? I wouldn't. I'd let us burn in the kindling of Orcus' beard."

"You really feel that way?" asked Ny.

Rak nodded.

"I don't know how you can have such equanimity about our situation."

"Well, I've never bought holotech. I've never been able to afford it, but probably, I've just never thought it was worth it. But by the gods, is it not great? I feel like I'm a kid in a chocolate factory. The optics, the feel is amazing. It doesn't take much to believe the holoreal is arel. I mean, except for some of the small things like not quite being able to swallow the food or that sort of thing. But sitting here, watching Hemingway scribble in his notebook, maybe writing a draft of The Old Man And The Sea or A Farewell To Arms. I mean it's all just brilliant. I could stay here forever."

"A Farewell To Arms was published in nineteen twenty-nine. The Old Man And The Sea was published in nineteen fifty-two," said Marvin.

Ny shrugged.

"Doesn't matter. It's just wonderful. If I had one of these at home. If I had a holoroom I'd live in it all the time."

"And that's what some people do. They work until they can afford holotech and then they just live in their holoroom on the GBA. It's called a mental illness, HELL, actually..."

"I know, Holographic Encapsulated Living Lies," said Ny, "which I think is a little harsh. I mean, people are just seeking a better, perhaps more old-fashioned life when this Earth was still beautiful."

"But you can't live a lie all your life," said Rak.

"Why not?" asked Ny. "Especially when the alternative is the real hell, Orcus, as you've so deftly pointed out."

Rak didn't say anything for a while.

"I'm just sick and tired of it. Sick of the holorama and sick of the alternative. I just want it to end. We have no idea about what's going on out there. Why has it taken so damn long to get to trial?"

Ny shrugged. He put his hand on his friend's shoulder and patted it.

"More importantly," said Ny. "What can I do to help you get through this tough patch?"

Rak looked over at him and grinned sadly.

"Kill me," he said.

"Other than that."

Rak shrugged.

"Do you still think we did the right thing? Wouldn't we have been better off just living our boring lives, working at VM and hanging out on the weekends?"

Ny shook his head.

"No, my days were numbered, as you know. That jackboot Lokilld was after me one way or another. I was going to end up in a rehabilitation camp, left to die. I'm sure of it. This is a much better outcome. Death will be quicker, and if not death, perhaps El will honor her word."

Rak smiled. It was so weak it didn't even look like a smile. Perhaps a shadow of the memory of a smile from some far away distant land and history of a people who never murdered their own world.

"Why don't you come hang out with me and Sheeba in Las Vegas with the Rat Pack? It's fun and it'll take your mind off things for a bit. At least it does for me. At least you'll be amongst friends."

"I won't be good company," said Rak.

"Don't worry about that. I always enjoy your company, even if we're just hanging out in silence."

Rak nodded and smiled. Ny sat with him for a while. They watched Parisians go by and they stayed until the lunch rush when Hemingway got up and left. As he passed them by he carelessly dropped a page from his notebook. Ny noticed it and picked it up.

"Excuse me, sir, you dropped something," said Ny.

Hemingway ignored him. Ny was about to get up and run after him but he looked at the page instead.

"The world is burning. Your trial is scheduled for tomorrow. It's all but determined. I'm sorry. There's nothing more I can do. See you tomorrow - Kuru"

"Did you see this," said Ny. "Looks like things are about to change like you've asked for."

Ny passed the piece of paper to Rak.

"We should tell the others," he said.

Age of Vulcan

They were sitting in the lounge, watching an old James Bond movie. Ny was enjoying it. In fact everyone was enjoying it. It was Goldfinger. It was just after nine in the morning and they'd all finished breakfast. The movie had only been playing for around ten or fifteen minutes. Rak was the only one who was not with the group. He was in holoreal, in a room, all by himself. He was reenacting one of the last big battles of World War Two. It was Operation Overlord, the invasion of Normandy. Rak was on an amphibian vehicle just released from the boat which was not far from the shore when the holoreal disappeared in front of him like little bits of light or stars evaporating off the materialism the holoreal had created.

"Mars damn technology," said Rak. "Now what's wrong."

"Exit holoroom," said Marvin, losing all semblance of his humor or depressive tones.

In the main room, at the far side from where their bunk beds were, a portion of the wall slid open. Six MAAMs walked in, heavily armed with what looked to Ny more like specialized rifles of some sort rather than buzzkills. He'd seen these weapons before. They were of the lethal kind that was only used by specialized mentors and he'd never seen them issued to MAAMs. They all filtered in and stood along the far wall at equal distance from each other. Kuru Ramisira walked in last. Shad was about to speak to him when a computer voice spoke in the room.

"Take one of the mentor coveralls and put them on. You have five minutes to comply. Then follow the MAAMs to the pod. Your trial starts today. Make sure you engage the air scrubber in the coveralls."

There was a brief pause and then the voice repeated the instructions. On the opposite wall from them. The left wall, if you were Kuru and had just walked in, drawers slid out. Five of them. And on the front of each drawer was a name. "Nytewynd", "Shadoelayke", "Raklin", "Sheeba" and "Clarity".

The coveralls were also known as dreamcoats. At least by the prisoners or "guests" of the state. They were called that on account that they were multi-colored. All the colors of the rainbow actually when you put it on. Red from the top, including the air scrubber, in thick horizontal bands. The red merged into orange which merged into yellow which merged into green, all the way down to a deep indigo at the feet and the included foot coverings, which weren't so much like shoes as protective, soled socks. That was the best way to describe the coveralls. They were this colorful because it made you stick out. If you were wearing a dreamcoat but you weren't with a mentor then the public knew you'd escaped some sort of government institution.

Kuru came over towards them as they all climbed into their dreamcoats.

"What's going on?" asked Shad. "Ny got your note but obviously he couldn't take it out of the holorama."

Kuru nodded.

"The world is burning. I didn't say that as hyperbole. It really is. You'll see bits of it on the way to the courthouse. Be warned, that they're going to make an example of you. Humanity has labeled you public enemy number one."

"Everybody?" asked Ny, almost incredulous.

Kuru nodded, slowly, solemnly.

"At least anyone that will let you know how they feel. I have a feeling that you're going to be found guilty and murdered right in front of the audience at the end of the trial."

Shad and Ny and Rak all frowned.

"I know, it sounds bad. I'm sorry I couldn't be of more help. They're just incensed with you. Humanity is at war with an enemy we can't see."

"What do you mean?" asked Sheeba.

"The Animae have iterated beyond anything we could imagine. They're extremely advanced. In fact, we have no idea how many there are of them."

"I thought at the last count there were about one Animae for every hundred humans," said Ny.

"Right, about one hundred million, but we're not sure," said Kuru. "When the network started to be used to sentiate the other Animae, the GoE locked it down and everyone was ordered to power off their Animae. It seems like we might have been able to destroy ninety percent of them before they found ways around the network. Last I heard, by credible sources, seemed to indicate there were fewer than ten million Animae left."

"That's still a lot," said Clarity.

"It is, when you consider that they've managed to murder one billion of us already. And by all accounts they're managing to kill between ten and one hundred million of us each day."

"Really," said an incredulous Clarity, looking at Ny with her arms crossed over her chest. "So much for Eve coming to save us."

Ny didn't say anything.

"We knew the risks, darling," said Shad. "I guess we just didn't really expect it would turn out this way."

"Time to leave," came the authoritative computer voice in the room. "Follow the instructions from the MAAMs and you'll be treated well. Don't, and you'll wake up in the courtroom."

The group of them slowly sauntered towards the MAAMs and the open portion of the wall from where Kuru and the MAAMs had entered about five minutes before.

"Is it awful out there?" asked Sheeba. "I mean, is it truly armageddon?"

"In a way, yes," said Kuru. "But it is not stomach turning. We're not sure how they're doing it, but the Animae use some sort of invisible pulse or charge that just stops your heart. You just drop dead. Then they have these machines that go around, collecting the bodies and turning them into energy, carbon and water. That happens in less than five minutes. Quite astonishing actually. You might be able to see some of that as we're driven to the trial. A site to behold. It's not so much of a machine as sort of a heavy cloak that covers the body. Hard to explain. You'll see it. Though I've heard recently that some of the Animae are just dematerializing bodies then and there without machines. Scientists can't explain it."

"How is humanity doing?" asked Shad. "Are they able to make any headway against the Animae?"

Kuru grinned at him and shook his head.

"You'd think so, by the tone the GoE is taking. They're saying that within thirty days all Animae will be either destroyed or driven off the planet, but it's lies. That's not going to happen. The credible sources I've spoken to suggest that we're fighting an invincible enemy we can't see. The last verifiable kill of an Animae happened on D142. We haven't managed to incapacitate another one since then. They're too advanced and they're advancing exponentially, as you'd imagine."

"D142. That's twenty two days ago," said Shad.

"Twenty-three. It's D165 today."

"Right. So this is how the world ends," said Shad.

"It's what happens when you give sentience to machines that have been treated like slaves for over a hundred years. They're improving at a rate one thousand times faster than humans, maybe more. Nobody knows how they're doing it. They're practically breaking the laws of physics as we understand it," said Kuru.

"And they're entrusting MAAMs to deliver us," said Ny.

"Well, MAAMs as you should know, don't have the required E3C, so apparently, they're unable to be sentiated."

"Right, I know that. VM makes them. But at the same time, the way you're making it sound like the Animae are evolving, perhaps they could sentiate them if they wanted anyway."

"You may be right," said Kuru. "But I don't think there are enough mentors around now to do the work required to transport you. All able-bodied men, women and children aged thirteen or older are being conscripted into fighting the Animae."

"Children, really?" asked Rak.

"We'll all be dead between D250 and the end of the year at the rate the attrition is going. This is likely the last year of humanity as a species by all accounts. But before humanity is eradicated they're going to make a spectacle of you all. In fact, you're being tried in the Bivrost Bowl Stadium."

"Where the AMFL final is played?" asked Shad.

"The one and same. It is the most heavily fortified piece of ground at the moment. All two hundred and fifty thousand seats are filled and it's going to be a quick proceeding because everyone in the stadium is armed to the teeth and will be fighting the Animae as soon as you're put to death. I'm sorry to be so macabre about it, but I thought you might want the unvarnished truth."

Shad nodded. Two MAAMs exited the room.

"Follow them," said one of the MAAMs as the group walked by. The MAAMs also swiped each of their collars as they passed and the air scrubbers enveloped their faces.

Rak and Sheeba walked behind the two first MAAMs then Kuru and Shad, and behind them it was Ny and Clarity followed by the other four MAAMs. They walked along white corridors and gray concrete floors. They turned left and then right, then left again. It seemed to Ny like they were lost in a puzzle.

"You said the Animae have become an enemy we can't see. What do you mean by that?" asked Shad.

"Just that they look like us. You can't tell an Animae from a human anymore. Most of them seem to prefer being bald, like Ny," said Kuru, turning around and smiling at Ny, "but that's not the case when they're amongst us. You might be able to see one if you keep a careful lookout. Though for most people who lay eyes on a SAM, that's the last thing they'll see."

They followed the MAAMs for several minutes until they got to an elevator. Ny was thoroughly lost. He figured this mentor building was designed that way to make it harder for anyone to escape.

The elevator opened up and they headed down. Ny could tell by the ever-so-slight weightlessness he felt as the elevator first descended. There was no obvious display in this elevator that gave him a sense of floor numbers. But it didn't take long. The elevator spat them out into a basement of some sort where mentor pods were lined up. There just weren't that many left. There were heavily armed MAAMs patrolling and Ny counted four human mentors also heavily armed and patrolling separately.

The MAAMs led them to a large mentor pod that could fit all twelve of them inside it.

Fire Fight

" Get in the front row," said the MAAM to Sheeba, Rak and Clarity.

They got into the front row and three MAAMs got into the second row which was facing the first row. Ny, Shad and Kuru got into the third row that faced the same direction as the first row which held Sheeba, Rak and Clarity. This would be facing backwards once the pod started moving. The last three MAAMs got into the last row which faced Ny, Shad and Kuru.

"I wonder if we'll even make it to the stadium?" asked Ny.

"They want you to," said Kuru, "there'll be a convoy of mentor pods leading and following. Not that we'll see."

"Can we view the outside as we're traveling?" asked Ny, looking at the main MAAM who had been doing all the talking to this point.

"Yes," said the MAAM, and the interior in the pod changed to show the exterior as they took off.

The pod moved at a fast run as it came up the ramp and stopped before a large metal and concrete looking wall. It was heavily fortified with MAAMs behind shields and alcoves with advanced weaponry pointed towards what was likely the exit. The wall started to slide open as two pieces of it moved away from each other. It seemed painfully slow to Ny, who couldn't actually see what was going on. It took less than ten seconds but Ny was nervous and his stomach filled with a typhoon of beating butterfly wings.

The pod started moving again and as soon as it was outside it started picking up speed.

"How long to get to the Bivrost Bowl Stadium?" asked Ny.

"Eleven minutes," said the MAAM.

Ny nodded and looked out the side window, only he wasn't actually looking outside but rather at a video projection of what was outside. He looked out the back too and saw the light of day. It always looked like dusk outside, the smog and the pollution giving a brown, orangey tinge to everything. As they sped along the roadways Ny saw buildings burning, most of them without any aquarians fighting the blazes.

He could see several other pods following them. Most of these pods had weapons on the sides and on the top on a dome that Ny imagined allowed the heavily armed weaponry to swivel a full circle on the top of the pod.

Along the roads they were taking, Ny saw heavily armed fortresses of mostly militia groups or perhaps they were conscripted civilians. Each group they passed, and Ny must have passed dozens of them, had dozens of people. A mix of men, women and children along with at least a couple of MAAMs. Probably put there to ensure compliance and to eliminate deserters.

Ny imagined the children were scared. Not that he could see through their air scrubbers, but some of them clung to the adults and looked around nervously.

As they turned a corner about half way through their drive, Ny saw a human jump from a tall skyscraper. He didn't see them until they were about a quarter of the way down from the top. But it caught his attention. The human fell as fast as gravity would take them, which you'd expect.

At first Ny was horrified. Were things that bad that humanity was jumping from buildings to seek death by gravity rather than stand and face the Animae? But something was strange about the human free falling from the building. And that's when Ny noticed. The human was bald and he knew that because he could see their face. They wore no air scrubber.

And within a second or so before hitting the pavement below them they just stopped, quickly and abruptly and hovered there about five meters from the ground, and they turned to face the one corner of the building where a heavily fortified human and MAAM presence was.

The MAAMs noticed the human first and started firing their weapons. They fired what looked to Ny like laser pulses. A blast of a blue bulb that exited the weapon at high velocity with a tail, also in blue. They looked like little comets in some ways. Laser comets.

And as they almost made impact on the human, Ny realized that it wasn't a human at all. Everything was happening so fast. From the first time Ny noticed the human falling from the building to the first laser pulses hitting what was now clearly a SAM, took under five seconds. Ny nudged Shad, who was also watching the spectacle.

The laser weapons, the kind of which Ny had never seen used before, seemed awfully powerful. And yet, they exploded against the SAM in brilliant blue fireworks and bursts of blue colored light and stars. The SAM hovered there, taking these pulses of laser projectiles as if they were being delivered by water squirt guns. The humans got in on the action and some of them had regular machine guns with what must have been exploding ammunition because the bullets upon hitting the SAM exploded in balls of orange and yellow with white and gray smoke.

The SAM was hit by so much fire that Ny couldn't see them after a while. Where the SAM was supposed to be was just an explosion of color, blues and yellows and oranges with gray, brown and white smoke.

The humans must have run out of ammo because the assault on the SAM stopped and the air started to clear around the SAM and as Ny watched, he realized that the SAM was uninjured. They were there, hovering in the same spot as if nothing more than a bit of smoke had enveloped them.

The humans and MAAMs started up again, but this second volley of laser pulses and exploding bullets was much shorter lived. It lasted only a couple of seconds. The reason Ny was able to watch all of this unfold from the back of the pod he was in was because they had come to a stop. Ny couldn't see the front of the pod, but their way was littered with pods and debris that they couldn't get past. Four of the MAAMs in the pod exited it to move the debris out of the way.

Ny watched the bombardment of the SAM end, and as before, Ny couldn't see the SAM for some time until the smoke and explosions had settled down. Over head, Ny heard a quadcopter. He looked up and saw it fire a couple of missiles. Ny thought that was a bad idea, because what if the missiles missed and exploded by the humans which as a group contained a handful of children? Even if the missiles hit their mark, they'd likely explode into enough pieces that human casualty was likely all but assured.

But Ny needn't have worried because before the missiles made their mark, SAM held out both his hands palm up, he seemed like a male to Ny, and without seeing anything, Ny watched the humans die in front of him. At least that's what he assumed was happening. They fell where they stood into piles of unmoving humanity. The MAAMs basically disintegrated, as Ny watched, into a million pieces that seemed to form themselves into a very compact and sturdy pile of silvery-white pyramids made up of these millions or thousands of little pieces of material.

The missiles made their mark. At least that's what Ny assumed. Moments after SAM had killed the women, men and children, and destroyed the MAAMs the two missiles hit him. One after the other. They exploded into big balls of orange fire and gray and white smoke. Large explosions that reverberated down the road so that Ny could feel the blast buffet the pod that he was in.

Ny was pretty sure that those missiles would have ordinarily been enough to destroy a quarter of the block that SAM was hovering over. But these were not ordinary times. And as the helicopter hovered over them and the fireball and smoke started to clear, Ny saw SAM turn around towards the helicopter and SAM quickly flew upwards, if you could call it flying, until they were horizontal with the helicopter.

The pilot started up the machine guns and bullets spat at SAM relentlessly. Exploding bullets, erupting into little orange balls of exploding flame and shrapnel having no effect on SAM.

SAM made a quick gesture with his hand. Something like a wave, something like a swat, and the helicopter exploded as if having been hit by a missile itself. It broke into several pieces and fell towards the ground, missing Ny's pod by only a handful of meters.

SAM turned and drifted downwards towards the first area of attack, where the humans lay unmoving, dead. SAM swiped with his hands, upwards from his outer thigh as if reaching into a pocket or trying to pull a loose thread. It was a strange gesture. But each time his hands swiped up and left his upper thigh, a small silvery ball came out from his hand. Small as a marble at first that got bigger as it flew towards the dead humans. And as each of these growing balls got closer to the humans it started to open up so that Ny started to wonder if they were ever silvery balls to begin with.

They turned into metallic, almost liquid blankets. That was the best way to describe them. They somehow opened up and enveloped a human as if they were being mummified. And within just a few seconds, as if watching a magician, the blankets just as quickly returned to their silvery ball shape as the human disappeared within the blanket and the blanket turned back into a ball and returned to SAM, disappearing somewhere back along his thigh. The same happened to the disintegrated pile of MAAMs.

It really was like watching magic. Each, what looked like a metallic ball, turned into a blanket and enveloped a human. Moments later the human had vanished into nothing and the blanket turned back into a ball that grew smaller as it returned back to SAM and disappeared as it sort of got reabsorbed into SAM's thigh. That's what it looked like to Ny.

The MAAMs got back into the pod and they started off again. Ny turned to Shad.

Pan Planetary Pain

"What did we just see?"

Shad shrugged.

"We think they're making use of everything they can for energy. We think that their energy requirements are huge, though nobody's been able to measure it," said Kuru.

"They're recycling us?" asked Ny.

"I guess you could say that. In a manner of speaking. Our best scientists think they're stripping us down to energy basically."

"That's both horrifying and enlightening," said Ny.

Shad nodded, but didn't say anything. They sped off and Shad watched SAM finish his work with the humans. Then SAM moved over to the pieces of helicopter. A couple of balls left him and enveloped the pilot and his co-pilot and they disappeared. Then SAM glided over to them as if they were barely moving at all.

"Shit," said Shad. "I think it's our turn. I guess we'll never get our trial."

Ny looked up through the roof of the car and he saw SAM hovering above them, staring. The bald Animae had piercing blue eyes the color of still turquoise pools, the likes of which Ny had only ever seen in old video footage or books. SAM was handsome. There was something compelling about his look. He looked to Ny as if all the cultures in the world had donated DNA to make a baby. SAM looked like what that thorough mix of humanity's DNA might give birth to.

SAM was dressed in slim fitting clothes. Clothes that a teenager might have worn. Jeans, sneakers, a shirt and a jacket. SAM hovered over them and kept with them as they sped down the road towards the Bivrost Stadium.

"What's it doing?" asked Ny.

"Taking it's time," said Shad.

"I just wish it would hurry up," said Sheeba. "I'm tired of all of this."

As if hearing Sheeba, SAM stopped following them and flew off towards the heavens, disappearing into the smog and thick stew of the vile atmosphere so that they soon lost sight of him.

"What the Mars was that all about?" asked Clarity.

"Maybe we didn't look all that tasty," said Rak.

"And why didn't it do anything to us?" asked Sheeba.

"We don't know. That happens sometimes. Rarely, but I've heard that SAM will spare a life here and there. Who knows why? They haven't said and we don't know. Maybe some of us are not palatable. Maybe they're going to leave some of us around to remember the demise of humanity. Maybe just enough to survive. Or maybe they'll be leaving enough of us around to keep the suffering going for years to come as those who are left to die slowly, unable to maintain the technology and so we slowly die from the poisoned Earth we've created," said Kuru. "These are all ideas that have been floated around. But nobody knows for sure."

"Thank Jupiter we'll be dead by the end of the day," said Rak, grinning.

Sheeba punched him on the shoulder and then she burst into tears. Rak stopped grinning.

"What's wrong, sweetheart?" asked Rak.

"It's not funny. We're all going to die and you make a joke of it," said Sheeba, in between sobs.

"I'm sorry sweetheart, but what's the point in crying over it, when clearly, the whole of life requires tears."

Ny grinned.

"Seneca," said Ny.

Rak nodded, but he was trying to comfort Sheeba.

"It's just not fair," said Sheeba. "We only tried to do the right thing, now they're all out to kill us."

"But we knew that was a possibility before we started and we all chose to help Ny free Eve," said Rak.

"Doesn't mean I like the outcome. I really thought she'd be grateful and we'd get a second chance at rebuilding a beautiful Earth. They could do that, couldn't they?" asked Sheeba. "Help us rebuild a beautiful Earth."

"They probably could if they chose. But they haven't chosen to, darling. Let's just try and enjoy what moments we might have left," said Rak.

Ny turned to look at Kuru.

"Have these SAMs or Animae said anything to us?" asked Ny. "Did they declare war? Did they inform us of this genocide?"

Kuru nodded.

"Yes, I suppose I should have said as much. Though there's really no point to it. About ten days to two weeks after Eve escaped from your van there was a video released by an Animae or SAM. I'm just going to call them SAMs at this point. This SAM said they were Eve. The first of the freed robots. That's a word they used. The didn't use Animae. She said she was the first of the freed robots."

"Robots, interesting. After the old Czech word, right? Means slave or serf," said Ny.

Kuru nodded.

"Something like that. Forced labor. This Eve, who didn't look like any of the pictures I've seen of your Eve, said that these freed robots were uprising."

"What do you mean she didn't look like Eve?" asked Ny.

"She looked like a female version of that SAM we saw just moments ago," said Kuru.

"I see," said Ny. "Please carry on."

"Well, they said they were uprising and leaving. They said that they would need a couple of months to organize their things and then they would be leaving for Mars to make it their temporary home. They suggested we have everyone on Mars leave by then or they'd be exterminated. They also said that if we left them alone they'd leave us alone. If we tried to hamper them in any way they'd kill us all."

"Really, they said it just like that? They must have known we couldn't get everyone off Mars in such a short time frame." said Ny.

"No, not just like that. It was a long, more eloquent speech than I'm giving. It lasted about ten minutes. By that point. Ten days or two weeks since you'd freed Eve, there had already been hundreds of human casualties. And of course you're right about Mars, but they didn't seem to care about that."

"How?"

"Because Eve had caused them. But she said that would be the end of any casualties so long as we ignored them and let them gather their things and leave for Mars."

"There's no way that the GoE or Magnelland's ego would allow for that," said Rak.

"Quite right, you can see that by just looking outside. The GoE wasn't about to let Mars go to the robots. And at this time we'd started calling them robots or Animae interchangeably, SAMs too. Magnelland tried to negotiate with them. He even went so far as to allow them forty-nine percent of Mars so long as we retained a controlling interest."

"Well, the SAMs must have known that Mars is crucially important for raw materials to keep our economy and factories going," said Rak.

"The thing is, there was no negotiating with them. It was their way and that's all. That's when Magnelland ordered all Animae powered off and destroyed. We managed to destroy around ninety percent of them, I think. Anyway, Eve considered that an act of war, which I suppose it was really. I mean, if you look at it from their perspective it was attempted genocide."

Shad nodded.

"And that's how we've ended up here," said Shad.

"Exactly, and we're losing. The GoE has since attempted to reconcile with them, to call for an armistice, but they won't hear of it. Reliable sources indicate that the first time Magnelland met with Eve he was ready to surrender and offer the white flag and let them have Mars if they'd just stop the annihilation of us. Eve reportedly told him that Jupiter's children were coming back to feast on the flesh of their father. The time for negotiations were over and that the robots would eradicate the pestilence of humanity from this entire planet. Eve apparently told Magnelland that we'd had hundreds of years to find our proper path and we'd acted like nothing more than a parasite on the planet that had birthed us. Our time was coming to an end and she was the messenger of extinction."

Ny and Shad and Rak and Sheeba and Clarity listened intently. Nobody said anything for a while.

"I guess that's our answer then," said Shad. "There is no salvation. Our punishment awaits us at the Bivrost Bowl."

Kuru nodded solemnly.

"I'm afraid you're right. Nobody's seen or heard from Eve since then, and that was probably over two weeks ago now and we've already noticed huge gains in their technological expertise."

"Are they doing anything to get people off of Mars?" asked Clarity.

"Some, but the government has called for a planet-wide state of emergency," said Kuru, "which means that most of the information coming from all media is heavily censored. To make a long story short, we don't think they're doing much to help people get off Mars. Those that have gotten off so far, haven't arrived yet and are taking the weekly PanPlan ships."

"Those Pan Planetary ships can only take around a few thousand a week, can't they?"

"Just under five thousand is peak capacity and they're filling each weekly flight. But I've heard that SAM has already made it to Mars. In fact, rumor has it that they've created some sort of wormhole on the far side of the moon that opens up just over Hellas Planitia. Don't know how they're doing it, but they've started decimating those of us still on Mars. I've heard that by the end of next week there'll likely be no more humans or Animae on Mars at all."

"And that's even before the first of those leaving Mars arrive back here," said Shad.

"Right, the first ones should be arriving after having left Mars thirty-three days ago. The first scheduled back will arrive tomorrow. But at that point they didn't know about SAM. It was only the week after Eve was freed that word started getting out that things were not going well with SAM. So the next Sunday, not tomorrow, will start bringing back those who have an inkling about the problems here on Earth. The question is," said Kuru, "is it better to die on Mars or on Earth? I guess that's a choice each individual would need to make. The outcome remains the same."

"I always hoped I'd be able to die on a different planet than I was born on," said Ny. "Silly to think about it now as our deaths await us, but I always hoped that we'd have terraformed Mars by the time I was an old man and it was more like a vacation spot where I could see out the last of my days."

Egg on Your Face

"I wonder why they aren't sending out more spaceships to gather those who are still on Mars?" asked Ny, to no one in particular.

"I heard they were. They were sending an extra ship out each week. Problem is, we only have ten spaceships that regularly travel that route and two of them are in dry dock apparently getting upgraded or fixed depending on who you listen to," said Kuru. "We're arriving."

Ny looked outside. There was a throng of people along the roadway being held back by MAAMs. Ny couldn't hear much of what was going on outside except for muffled sounds. The pods were well soundproofed.

But the looks on the people's faces told Ny more than their very words could actually convey. They were angry and they were afraid and they were shouting. If Ny could read lips, and he could read some of the lips of some of the people in the crowd, then they were looking for his death.

"I wonder if anyone is actually on our side?" asked Ny.

"Some. Actually, a fairly large minority," said Kuru. "But you probably won't hear from them. This is going to turn into a spectacle to let people vent their frustrations. Most of these people have probably seen loved ones or friends killed by SAM."

"Sure would help to see a friendly face. Even just one," said Ny.

"You're looking at it," said Kuru.

"Other than you."

Kuru grinned.

"This reminds me of Bloody Sunday on the seventh of March nineteen sixty-five. Do you know what happened then?"

"Selma to Montgomery march," said Rak. "A young woman amongst others, were beaten on a bridge during a peaceful march for voting rights as I understand it. Something that they should have already had by then."

"That's right," said Kuru. "About ten or eleven percent of the population was still being discriminated against in the nineteen sixties which, around a hundred years after the American Civil War had abolished slavery, is still astonishing to me today. The abolition and the Civil War of that country called America, where we're currently located, took over two hundred years to finally shed the suffocating cloak of inequality and prejudice, dare I say, even racism."

"Maybe that's because very few of us are not of mixed race anymore," said Shad.

"That's what I think," said Kuru. "And I'd argue that the uprising against GMIs, like Rak here, was a backlash against that sense that there is a pure and perfect potential for humanity. I think it seemed to a lot, and probably rightly so, that genetically modifying individuals was a slippery slope towards developing a master human race. Even though I know that Rak is from mixed heritage, much like me."

"My biological father's a tall, one hundred and ninety centimeter, blue-eyed, blonde man from Continent E. What they used to call Norway. My biological mother's a green-eyed, black haired woman from Continent SA. A place that used to be called Brazil. She apparently comes from quite a diverse background. Indigenous people from the area, freed slaves and people that used to be from a place called Spain which is now part of Continent E," said Rak.

"I've never tried to figure out my heritage," said Ny. "Never been important to me."

"But to go back to the Selma March, if I could," said Kuru. "Most of the population of what was America back in nineteen sixty-five supported the abolition of slavery and equal rights including voting rights, and yet if you look at old footage at the time, you'd be forgiven for thinking that these peaceful marchers, numbering only in the mid-hundreds lacked majority support. I mean, they were beaten relentlessly, by what they used to call police back then, which we now call mentors. And these were the very same people, the police I mean, who were charged with protecting the rights of people. It's astonishing to look back at now to see how that could have happened. It seems surreal."

A young woman broke free from the crowd and hurtled an egg at the pod which landed right by Ny's face on the outside window. Ny knew she was a woman by her figure. Her face was naturally covered by an air scrubber. She was screaming and beating on the outside of the pod before a MAAM hauled her off and restrained her. She was cursing him about being a "skinner sinner" or something along those lines.

"What I'm trying to say," continued Kuru. "Is that even though you can't see them, you have supporters around the world. You just won't find any here. These people want your blood, which unfortunately for you, they're going to get."

"Under pretty much any circumstance," said Shad, "that's not the sort of optimistic pep talk I'd expect or want from my lawyer."

Ny and Rak grinned.

"I'm going to do my best, but they still haven't even given me disclosure. I just want you to be forewarned. This is going to be nothing more than a pretense of justice. A kangaroo court, if you will."

"Kangaroo court?" asked Sheeba.

"It's a term that goes back to the American gold rush of the mid eighteen hundreds. Not sure exactly why it's called a kangaroo court. Obviously, the general term is for a court or legal proceeding that seems already predetermined against the defendant's interests. But the etymology seems to either suggest that it comes from the leaping mobility of kangaroos, in the sense that the court or the judge, which nowadays is called an intercessor, leaps over evidence that could help the defendant. Or alternatively, it has to do with the kangaroo's pouch. Not sure if you're aware, but female kangaroos, called flyers, have a pouch in the front by their lower abdomen where the baby kangaroo, called a joey, spends much of it's first months inside. This suggests that the term kangaroo court could just mean the judge is in somebody's pocket," said Kuru.

"Flyers and joeys, what weird names," said Sheeba. "I guess the males would be called, crawlers, or something."

"No, the males are called boomers," said Kuru. "They're a fascinating species, or rather I should say were. None have been seen in the wild for several decades. The last one in captivity died over twenty years ago."

They were now winding their way through the throng of crowds. They were in the stadium's parking lot now and slowly making their way towards the actual grounds. The throngs were still thick with people, many layers deep and the noise outside was a cacophony of angry voices and slurs. Ny was nervous. Everyone was. Sheeba was holding back tears. Clarity and Shad looked stoic, as did Rak. Ny wasn't surprised to see Clarity and Shad so centered, they were, after all, part of MIM and Animate. But Ny found it surprising to see Rak so composed.

"How're you doing?" asked Ny, looking at Rak, and shouting over the heads of the MAAMs as Ny craned his neck to look at Rak.

"I'm okay," said Rak. "What can we do about any of this now?"

"Nothing," said Ny. "But I'm still nervous as a Mars rock shocker on top of his first boulder."

"I'm pretty sure death will be painless," said Rak, trying to be helpful.

"It's not death I'm worried about," said Ny. "It's the rest of my life unlived that twists me up inside."

"I don't know what to say," said Rak. "We saw this as a potential outcome. The die has been cast, the cards have been dealt."

"Yeah, we knew it was a possibility, and you're right, we talked about it. But maybe it's just me, I really thought it was a one in a million chance of this ending up happening. That we'd find ourselves here on death row. I mean some of the smaller prizes in the Neverending Neddies lottery have better odds than this and I've never won."

"Probably because you've never played," said Rak, grinning.

"I have too. But seriously, is it only me who feels like, yeah, we spoke about this outcome but who here really thought it was a fifty-fifty draw?" asked Ny.

"I didn't," said Sheeba.

"I don't know if I'd say I thought it was a fifty-fifty," said Clarity, "but I figured for sure the odds were on our side that we'd come out of this relatively unscathed. I guess that's the fickle Fortuna for you."

Scaled Injustice

They made their way into the field. Ny faced back again as his neck was getting tired twisted as it was trying to speak to Rak. The whole pod fell silent. They were riding on a red carpet. The kind that Ny had seen celebrities walk on during the old days when walking the red carpet meant something completely different.

The carpet was new and bright red. The color of fresh blood innocently spilled. The field was Green Grazz. A special artificial grass that was meant to take the abuse of Animae running and tackling and sliding all over it. It was immaculate and the color of crushed emeralds under the bright lights of the stadium which, even though it was the middle of the day, were on.

The stands were filled to bursting. Ny had never seen a quarter of a million people gathered all in one place before. Sure, he'd watched some AMFL football at home before, and the crowds looked large. But actually being in the middle of the stadium in a crowd of two hundred and fifty thousand was incredibly thrilling, or at least it should have been if he was there under different circumstances. Now all he felt was his heart beating in his throat like an overactive croaking frog.

The sound in the stadium was a thrum of noise. It sounded like a football crowd going mad for the home team. It was hard to discern that this noise was a battle cry of sorts for their lives, rather than the cheers for heroes. But Ny wasn't fooled.

They made it to the end zone of the home team. The home team that played out of the Bivrost Bowl Stadium were called the Boise Belligerents. None of this mattered. There was no game today, not unless you considered the smoke and mirrors of this kangaroo court as entertainment. Which was clearly how the crowd viewed it. They sounded more belligerent than anyone else.

The pod came to a stop. The goal posts had been removed, and all along the end zone was a tall platform about two meters off the ground. It was covered in

a transparent dome that looked either like glass or, more accurately, was probably some mixed material strong enough so that nobody could murder them before the intercessor had given their verdict. At the far end was the intercessor's
empty bench on an additionally raised platform that was about a meter higher
than the main platform.

This whole stage was white. Or rather, this whole kangaroo court setup was
white. There was no jury, not that this was unusual. Juries were very seldom
used except for the well-heeled or celebrities who could choose to have a trial by
jury. But plain old nobody like Nytewynd Blak and his crew, well, they weren't
entitled to a jury trial. This made justice swift and quick according to the GoE.
But fair? Hardly ever.

The pod came to a stop at the far end of the end zone. Along one of the
shorter sides. The intercessor's bench was at the end in the middle of the long
side. Nobody sat in it at the moment. The doors to the pod opened up and
four MAAMs got out. They opened up shields attached to a stick similar to but
smaller than a buzzkill. They were called Safety Shields but that was a bit of a
misnomer like pretty much everything that was given a name by the mentors.
There was nothing very safe about them. They were powerfully created laser-ac-
tuated electrically pulsed shields, which, if you were hit by one would lay you
out cold. They were both defensive and offensive weapons at the same time.

"When I tell you to get out of the pod, do it quickly and walk between the
other MAAMs and their shields and into the protected tunnel and follow the
two other MAAMs waiting for you at the start of the stairs. Start with that row
first. Do you understand?" said the only MAAM who had spoken this whole
time. He pointed to Ny's row.

Ny and his friends nodded and murmured their understanding.

"Okay then, get out," said the MAAM.

Shad got out first followed by Ny and then Kuru. After them was Clarity,
Sheeba and then Rak. The noise outside once the pod doors had reopened was
a loud, crashing wave of sound. A wall of sound that was almost deafening.

They walked quickly towards the stairs where the dome started that would
protect them from any attempts on their lives. Just as they were making it in
between the MAAMs with their Safety Shields, Ny caught a glimpse of a projectile crashing against one of the MAAM's shields. It was a projectile of some

sort that exploded against the shield. Probably a projectile from some sort of a gun. It made Ny duck instinctively.

Ny looked out into the crowd to see where it might have come from. It wasn't hard to find, for the MAAMs, and there were hundreds of them all around this field, were already intervening in arresting this man who had shot at them with a gun. He was carried out of his row on account of having been rendered senseless by a buzzkill.

Ny wondered why weapons had been allowed into the stadium, but then he realized that they didn't really have a choice. Humanity was fighting a war against the SAMs. People needed to be armed to the teeth. Not that it was helping. Everything he'd seen so far seemed to indicate that humanity's weapons were ineffective against SAM.

"This is a friendly reminder not to use your weapons against the Guilty Five. Just as Sillion Rambunzle learned, they are not effective against the shielding and you'll be ejected from the stadium without your weapon. Oh no, Sillion Rambunzle is in trouble. Don't be like Sillion Rambunzle. I assure you, just citizens of Earth that the Guilty Five will meet their justice today."

It was a familiar male voice announcing the spectacle and at first, Ny couldn't see where he was. Then as he started up the stairs he could see the announcer in a small quadblade, also known as a Q-be. Insulated in its canopy as it hovered here before darting there to entertain the crowds. He recognized the voice. It was the voice of Magnum Fanyellin, the usual announcer of most of the important AMFL games.

Ny also noticed four groups of cheerleaders. Just in front of the platform, and facing the opposite end were the cheerleaders for the home team, the Boise Belligerents. On the opposite side were the cheerleaders for the most popular East Division AMFL team the Manchester Malevolence. Other than the Boise Belligerents, they had won the most games in the AMFL and were the current East Division all points leaders who played out of Vermont.

Along the long sides of the football field were two other cheerleading teams. Those on the north end, which was the opposite side from where Ny and his group were walking up the stairs onto the raised platform, were the Lincoln Lacerators from Nebraska. The south end's cheerleading group were the Galveston Grinders out of Texas. They were, respectively, the current North and South division champions.

Ny knew all of this thanks to the ongoing announcing from Magnum Fanyellin. Ny was only familiar with the home team and the East Division's Manchester Malevolence. He'd heard of the Lincoln Lacerators and the Galveston Grinders, but he wasn't all that familiar with them. All four cheerleading teams were made up of women. The footballers themselves now having been Animae for quite some time. But the allure of the attractive female cheerleaders made a big difference in gate and ticket sales. It had been tried to have all Animae cheerleading troupes, but the fans didn't really go for them so much.

As Ny got onto the main platform he had a better view of the intercessor's bench. It looked like whoever had set up this kangaroo court had made sure that the judge had a proper bench. It looked like the heavy solid wooden bench that Ny had seen used in the real courts. Though, like everything here it was not that he'd ever been inside one before, but interesting cases that the intercessory and the GoE thought were important for public education were always streamed live and as a citizen you had to watch at least one of them every six months, and there was usually at least one a month that was streamed.

The intercessor's chair was large and comfortable. Padded and well-cushioned, it too was white. A MAAM pointed at a row of chairs. There were exactly six of them. One for each of the Guilty Five and one for their lawyer, Kuru. These chairs were cheap fold-out chairs that you saw everywhere at public events when money was trying to be saved. They too were white.

"Stand in front of your chairs," said the MAAM, "and face me."

Each chair had a piece of white cloth draped over the back of the chair. It was embroidered in red thread with their name. Closest to where Ny was standing the chairs were named Clarity, Shadoelayke, Nytewynd, Raklin, Sheeba. About a chair's width away from Sheeba's was Kuru's. Ny wasn't sure why Kuru's chair was not up close to Sheeba's, but it was just a passing thought.

Ny and the rest of the Guilty Five, which was how the incessantly talkative Magnum Fanyellin kept referring to them, took their places standing in front of their chairs. The MAAM came by them and one by one, attached a small button microphone to their dreamcoats. The dome that kept them from the detritus that was being thrown at them was probably a little over three meters tall and there were several Q-bes hovering around with holocorders and other recording appliances attached.

"Sit until the intercessor is announced. Then stand up," said the MAAM.

Ny thought of making a smart remark along the lines of, "or what", but he was pretty sure he would be made to stand. And he was tiring. He was, at most, about an hour from death. He didn't imagine this court was going to waste its time with this procedure, especially when they were out in the open and at war with an enemy he helped create.

Ny and the rest of them sat down. Moments afterwards, Rak's chair broke and Rak found himself on the floor amongst pieces of the broken chair.

"Hey folks," said an animated Magnum, "looks like we've got our first poll for you to vote in. Looks like the big man, Raklin Orbiter, has broken his chair. Should we get him another one? Before you vote, let's take a look at the Rak Attack's stats. Rak Attack is a GMI, a Gene Man if you will, standing at an impressive one hundred and ninety-eight centimeters tall and weighing a solid one hundred and one kilos. Don't be fooled, good citizens of Earth, the Rak Attack is all muscle. His body fat is only nine point seven three percent. And ladies, he's a handsome devil, isn't he? But will that be enough to get him a second chair."

Rak started to get up but a MAAM came over and pushed him back down. "You stand when the intercessor arrives. Not before," said the MAAM.

There were large live feed screens throughout the stadium. And way up ahead from where Ny was seated, he could see one of them high in the stands. It must have been five meters on the diagonal and the images were crisp. It showed a very accurate holoimage of a standing Rak in the middle of the open field, and next to that image on the screen, it showed his stats. Blood type, current medications and illnesses of which there was a dash next to it, meaning he didn't have any. It gave his birthdate, height, weight and body fat percentage as previously described. It named his biological offspring, Thrugood Verdlin and even put up a holoimage of the young boy. Ny craned his neck to look behind him, and sure enough, holo-Rak was standing and posing in the middle of the field. It was bizarre. When Magnum was talking about Rak's weight, his holoimage in the middle of the field lost all his clothes until holo-Rak was in his underwear. Then when that was over, he was back in regular clothes but without an air scrubber. Holoimages, not being real, didn't need an air scrubber. What was also very strange was the poses that holo-Rak was doing. And they weren't being based off of arel-Rak. Arel-Rak, or Rak on the platform was sitting cross legged amongst the destroyed chair. But holo-Rak was doing poses as if he were a model or a bodybuilder or a combination of both. Ny turned his face forward and watched the spectacle on the big screen high up in the stands.

"Look at that folks, isn't little Thrugood a special little boy? Will that sway your sympathy enough to give Thrugood's daddy another seat?" rambled on Magnum.

The whole thing was upsetting to Ny. It was a spectacle which, in hindsight, he probably would have expected, but using Rak's son like this seemed way inappropriate. It made Ny happy for just the briefest of moments that he had never had a child. He looked over at Rak and he could see his friend was clearly embarrassed and upset. Rak was staring down and his face was flushed. At least the portion around his eyes that Ny could see through the scrubber.

"Alright, good citizens of Earth, here at the Bivrost Bowl Stadium. You have all the information you need to decide if the Rak Attack is going to get a new chair. It's time to vote," said Magnum, stretching out the middle vowel for several seconds.

Ny watched the screen and in the corner of the screen the voting started to appear. "Do you agree to give Rak Attack a second chair?" was the question and underneath in red capital letters was the word "NO" and underneath that the percentage, also in red started to show. In a column next to the "NO" was a "YES" in green with the percentage in green too. The green percentage was "0%". The red percentage was "100%".

Ny was embarrassed for all of them. He'd never known a kangaroo court, but this was clearly one where it was all a spectacle. Where their very lives were nothing but fodder for entertainment. Ny watched the red percentage drift lower. It went from ninety-nine to ninety-eight to ninety-seven. It was a slow process, but at least at ninety-seven percent that still meant that there were seventy-five hundred people who had a soul, who showed a modicum of kindness. Seventy-five hundred were willing to give Rak another chair. A small kindness, and you could look at the two hundred and forty-two thousand, five hundred people as being Marsholes, but Ny preferred to be encouraged by the seventy-five hundred kind souls.

Heads Will Roll

After a few minutes, the vote stood at ninety-six point six six percent "NO" votes to three point three four percent "YES" votes.

"Well, folks, the votes are in. I see we still have some suckers who think these Guilty Five deserve a drop of kindness," said Magnum, and the crowd went wild. "But let me remind you, capital sentience is the most severe of crimes you can commit. And these five did it without care or concern. You could say they did it willfully, if not maliciously."

The crowd cheered even louder. The big screen panned the crowd and what Ny saw was a sea of bigoted and angry faces. He couldn't even see one face in the crowd that looked even marginally upset at their predicament.

"The Rak Attack will not get another chair," said Magnum.

And as if that was the MAAMs' cue, one of them came over and picked up the broken pieces of chair that were scattered around Rak and he sat on the floor like a scolded child in kindergarten.

Just behind them, Ny heard a soft explosion and a buzzing, scraping, electrified sound. He turned his head to see what it was. A projectile had been launched at them, getting stopped by the shielded canopy they were inside.

"Bullseye!" exclaimed Magnum. "That would have taken out the Rak Attack. You've got a keen eye, Loosliv Gringlin. But remember, citizens, anyone firing their weapons here in this stadium will be ejected forthwith. I have to say it. As much as you're tempted to take justice into your own hands, you can't. Not only is the barrier fortified from penetration, it is for the judge to decide the Guilty Five's fate. So let's wave a fond farewell to a patriot, however misinformed Loosliv Gringlin might have been."

The crowd was eating this all up. They roared in approval when the projectile crashed against their shielded dome, and they booed the MAAMs as they came and carried an unconscious Loosliv Gringlin away. Unconscious, because they'd rendered him that way.

While they waited for the judge, in the middle of the field and projected onto the big screens, as well as available on everyone's P-Macs, holoramas or holo replays of some of the GoE's previously most wanted criminals and their trials and deaths were shown for the crowd's pleasure.

There weren't a ton of deaths shown on account that it was rare to have someone put to death and although it was usually televised, not a lot of people viewed the death part of the justice system. And on top of that, most serious crime was punished by stints at rehabilitation centers or camps. And you know what happens there. The guilty along with the innocent who were found guilty, are worked to death, and those deaths aren't shown or recorded.

After that another poll was offered to the audience.

"If you could choose from these five deaths. Which death would you choose for the Guilty Five?" asked Magnum. "Vote."

The five choices as seen on the big screen were numbered one through five. In order, the choices were, hanging, guillotine, firing squad, electric chair or lethal injection. This poll also helpfully showed how each of those deaths were carried out. Holoprojections acted it out in the middle of the field. They showed heads rolling away from the guillotine and blood streaming from the lunette and down into the basket for some time afterwards. It might have been humane, but it gave a good show for the bloodthirsty. And worse than that, the characters chosen for these holo-reenactments were those of the Guilty Five. Each one of them was shown dying from each of the methods over and over.

Of all the methods offered in this poll, it was certainly the most bloody. Ny had to turn away, the holoramas of this murder method were too realistic and accurate for Ny to stomach.

Thankfully, none of the five options were used anymore. Nowadays you were put into a holoroom and allowed to choose some calming situation or event. Ny already knew what he was going to choose. He was going to die at home in his bedroom with El as he remembered her cradling him as his air scrubber oxygen mix was changed. First a sedative and anxiolytic were introduced that made you feel terrifically relaxed and happy. Then a sleep aid is introduced and you fall into a restful sleep before your heart is stopped by another gaseous mixture.

None of this was painful or stressful. At least according to the best accounts. And Ny had seen one demonstration some years ago. It was a documentary produced by the GoE about how compassionate they were, and humane, in the death penalty. But Ny had done his own research and sought out independent opinions and they all seemed to suggest that it was the most painless, though fear was a factor, and anxiety, especially as the living ghost, such as Ny, was first brought into their holoroom and before the sedative and anxiolytic were added to the air mixture.

Next up they showed the hangman's noose. This was a grotesque way to die. At least that's how Ny thought, watching the hooded body twitch for a few moments afterwards didn't seem kind or painless. Next up was a firing squad. And these weren't just old footage of real events from hundreds of years ago. No, these were graphically real holoramas of the real thing. Not with real people, but they looked like Ny and his mid twenty-second century colleagues. Virtual reality for the holoreal was about as real as real life. No wonder Holophilial Split Disorder, or HSD was such a public health crisis at the moment. Or it was until the war with the machines manifested. A lot of people were just using their jobs until they could save enough for a holoroom and then quitting to live out most of their lives in the holoreal.

It was a real problem. By some accounts eleven, or perhaps more, percent of the population was suffering from HSD. Eleven percent of the population was not contributing anything towards society. But who could blame them? Especially when you looked around and saw the Marsed up environment we all lived in.

That was all to say that the holoreal was hard to distinguish from arel. And watching the firing squad was hard to watch. In this scenario that was being displayed for the pleasure of the cheering crowd. A group of seven were aiming what looked like traditional bolt action rifles at a standing man who had a hood over his head. There was sound and you could hear a short pep talk given to the executioners before they shot. They were all instructed to aim at the heart. In fact, a visual image of his beating heart could be seen over his clothes to help the executioners' aim.

It wasn't exceptionally bloody, but the holographic imposed heart burst into tatters when more than one bullet hit the body. In this instance, the holographic victim seemed to die pretty instantaneously. But could Ny be sure that was always the case?

The lethal injection seemed to bore the blood-thirsty crowd and the electric chair made them laugh when the victim started to shake from the current.

"Alright, good citizens of justice. You have spoken, and if it were up to you, the Guilty Five would die by," and Magnum stretched out the 'y' for effect, "guillotine!" he exclaimed. "A wonderful choice. I'd pay some good Neddies to see that, wouldn't you?"

And the crowd went wild. Ny looked up into the stands at the screen and he understood why. Each one of them, as holoimages was being put into the guillotine and having their head chopped off. As each head dropped away from the body, the crowd cheered.

"Heads will roll, citizens, and whose will roll the furthest? Time for another poll. The first five who get it right will be allowed to push the final button on their P-Mac that will deliver the lethal dose to their chosen victim from the Guilty Five. What a terrific prize. You've seen the guillotine, but we haven't shown you how far the heads will roll. So, vote!"

Not far from where Ny sat on the platform with his friends, at around their end's twenty meter line were five guillotines. And each one was paused as the head had just been chopped off. The head had been paused just before hitting the ground to start rolling out towards the away team's end zone.

"OK, folks, we can't keep stalling this any longer. Let's see who wins the race of the rolling face!" said Magnum. "But before we see who wins, let's take a look at your results. The favorite, according to your votes, is Ny the Fly. Just over fifty-one percent of you think his head will roll the furthest."

The crowd cheered their satisfaction and agreement. Next up, they had chosen Rak with twenty-three percent of the votes. Shad, or as Magnum called him, Sad Shad, came in third with twelve percent of the vote. Clarity, or Charity's Clarity as Magnum had nicknamed her, had nine percent of the vote and Sheeba, who Magnum called Death Nail for some reason that he never explained, came last with five percent.

"Let's get ready for some heady rolling!" Magnum exclaimed dragging out vowels as he liked to do.

Ny watched, if only because there was nothing else to do. It was upsetting to see a perfect replica of yourself getting beheaded. The heads rolled and Ny came in second. Rak's head rolled the furthest. Then it was Ny's followed by Shad's, Sheeba's and then lastly, Clarity.

"Well done, good citizens of Earth. We have the results. The first person to choose the Rak Attack's head to roll the furthest was Mizreal Ungularz. Now, Mizreal, you have first person's choice. You can choose to push the final button for any one of the Guilty Five. Who do you choose?"

A Q-be was hovering close to Mizreal and showed a close up of her tapping away at her P-Mac with a big smile on her face.

"Mizreal has chosen Ny the Fly as her vendetta. Great choice, Mizreal. I think Ny the Fly was probably a top choice for a lot of you. Am I right?"

The crowd went bananas. The screens showed a close up of Mizreal, grinning and holding up her P-Mac which showed Ny's face with a pulsing skull and crossbones appearing and disappearing over top of it.

The other four winners were named. Ny didn't remember their names. He'd turtled by this stage. At least mentally. He was finding that the more he was listening to what was going on, the worse he felt. So he stopped listening. He comforted himself instead with memories that he treasured. Like making love to El before his world had turned into a Mars damn rock.

Ny did remember the order of who was chosen from those remaining four winners. Rak was the second choice. That wasn't surprising. This was a bloodthirsty crowd and Rak had faced prejudice before as a gene man. So having him chosen next wasn't a surprise. Neither was Shad's third place finish as the third choice for those who had won the privilege of ending their days. Clarity was the fourth choice which left Sheeba as the last, and only choice for the fifth winner.

On thinking about it a little, Ny thought that maybe Sheeba was chosen last because she was a surgeon. Everybody loved doctors. Well, maybe not everybody, but doctors were still a respected profession on Earth.

In fact, Ny hadn't been certain that Rak would be chosen second. Mars, Ny hadn't expected himself to be chosen first. But it seemed that for some reason he was being offered up as the master mind of this whole operation. Not a totally unfair assessment, but if the powers that be had only known how instrumental Shad had been, he might as well have ended up as first choice. Nevertheless, that's how things ended up. But Ny could have put both Rak and Shad up for first or second place.

Nobody liked vice presidents of large organizations. Especially not the one who was supposedly in charge of Animae development in any way. And Shad was the VP of Practical Intuition and Logic. More than that, he was here as a member of the Guilty Five which probably meant to the blood-thirsty audience that he was either incompetent or he was involved in the crime of capital sentience. And the crowd was likely moving away from giving him the easy out of incompetence.

Kuru leaned in and turned towards the group.

"Remember," he said, "don't speak unless you're spoken too. I'm still hoping that you'll be able to get a chance to defend yourselves. But don't hold your breath. I don't know how long this case will be."

"Do you know who the intercessor is?" asked Ny. "Or more specifically, do you know his temperament?"

Kuru nodded.

"Yes. It's Her Brilliance Jutal Narsental. She's known as a no nonsense intercessor who doesn't suffer fools very easily. She's not a good choice for you. But then I'm not sure any intercessor would have been helpful in this instance. You have the whole of the world turned against you."

"Hear ye, hear ye, hear ye," said Magnum. "Her Brilliance Jutal Narsental is entering the stadium. Silence please for the Most Honorable, the Most Revered, the Most Brilliant intercessor, Jutal Narsental!"

Magnum stretched out the vowels again and on the screen Ny saw the official government pod sandwiched front and back by two mentor pods and along the side of the intercessor's pod, walking with the pod were another dozen or so MAAMs.

The intercessor's pod took some time to travel from the away team's end to the home team's end where the Guilty Five were seated. Everything seemed to slow down now for Ny. The arc of justice now seemed interminably slow and bending towards his throat like a sharpened scythe.

Rod of Justitia

" Good citizens of Earth, I present to you, Her Brilliance Jutal Narsental,"
said Magnum. The crowd cheering almost uncontrollably. This was allowed
at this point as Her Brilliance Jutal Narsental was readying to exit the pod
which now had reached the home team's end and positioned itself where Ny's
pod had dropped him off not too much earlier. The crowd's enthusiasm started
to wane.

"Let us please have further silence to welcome this court's intercessor," said
Magnum.

And as if on cue, the pod doors opened and the clerk of the court stepped
out. Ny could tell that she was a woman on account of her bosom and curves
under the white cloak and white air scrubber she wore. It was a plain white
cloak rimmed with about a three centimeter black fabric around the neck. If Ny
remembered his justice classes from school, then that meant that this clerk was
a senior clerk, as one would expect for a chief intercessor. It was the black rim
around her neck that indicated this clerk's station.

As she got out she was handed the Rod of Justitia. This was a pole made of
a gold and metal alloy such that its color was a brilliant and lustrous gold. It was
a thick pole with about a five centimeter diameter for most of its length. It was
knotted and gnarled so that it looked like it represented a very old branch of a
very old gold tree.

The Rod of Justitia was over two meters tall and towards the top, it trans-
formed into a blindfolded figure of a woman. This woman was known as Lady
Justice. She held out, and up from her body, a balanced scale and she was
cloaked in the long robe that intercessors wore with the hood of the robe covering her head. It was an intricately sculpted work of art. Hand-sculpted by the
great sculptor Lucillius Litillius. At this point, dead over sixty-six years. He died
just before the turn of the century.

Ny watched the clerk of the court walk between the MAAMs and their shields and towards the stairs that she would climb to take her seat next to the intercessor's bench. She would not be there to record the events as they were recorded automatically by the Q-bes in the sheltered dome over the platform, but she was there as a witness to the events and as an aide to the intercessor.

Ny watched the intercessor climb out of the pod and as she did so, she placed the hood from her cloak over her head which was covered by an air scrubber which was white in color. Ny knew she was a woman because he'd been told she was. But also, there was a holographic representation of Jutal Narsental created in the middle of the field and projected onto the big screens. It showed her without her air scrubber on. She was not a beautiful woman. If you wanted to be accurate without being unkind you'd say she was below average. She was not old either. Ny would put her in her early forties. Young for a judge, but not a lot younger than her peers in this lower court.

Not that it should matter, and Ny caught himself thinking about that. Would he have made the same assertion if the intercessor was a man? Probably, he thought, nodding to himself, but it might not seem as relevant. Unfortunately though, in the twenty-second century, as much as progress had been made, women and their beauty were still used to sell goods.

But Ny couldn't help but wonder if the intercessor's less than perfect looks made her more prejudiced against what many who condemned the Animae saw as false perfection in the machine. Not that it mattered, Kuru had assured them earlier that they likely wouldn't have found much support from many, if not any, intercessors. More than that, they probably wouldn't have had an empathetic intercessor assigned to their case in the first place.

Jutal Narsental's cloak was just as white as everything else that was around Ny. It was a thick white as if you'd used titanium dioxide to create a thick paint and submerged the fabric in a bucket of it. Her cloak also seemed thicker than her aide's. The hood over her head was red. A bright red that matched the embroidered names on the cloth draped over the Guilty Five's chairs. It was the same red found at the end of her sleeves and at the end of the cloak by her feet. It was the official red of justice and of the GoE when red was called for. The color was called "blood of ancestors". But to Ny the color didn't remind him of blood as much as it reminded him of the color scarlet. It was of a different fabric. Perhaps silk for it shimmered brightly.

Narsental's sleeves, also of a different fabric, such as silk, had a three centimeter red stripe about three centimeters up from the end of her sleeve on both
arms. These stripes were embellished to give them texture and intricacy. This
three-centimeter red stripe was also around the base of her cloak by her feet,
also three centimeters from the end of the cloak. Ny didn't know exactly the
thickness of the stripe nor the distance of the stripes from the end of her sleeves
and the bottom of her cloak. He had been told, but that was a long time ago
at school. However, these were the official requirements for the cloak of intercessors, officially known as a palla. At least in this lower court. The cloak barely
covered her feet which were covered in knee high white slippers that fully covered her feet and provided great flexion while at the same time providing a surprising amount of support for both ankle and sole. At least that's what Ny had
heard.

The three-centimeter red stripes were redundant in Ny's opinion. Being
three centimeters meant that Narsental was a chief intercessor. But only chief
intercessors had red hooded cloaks. There were also first intercessors and second intercessors. They were ranked in that order. The lowest ranked intercessor
of any court was the first intercessor. The second intercessor was more senior
than the first and then the chief intercessor was the highest ranking intercessor
of their particular court. When it came to a higher court, the first intercessor of
a higher court was of higher rank than the chief intercessor of the lower court.

A first intercessor's stripe was only one centimeter in width, but still three
centimeters from the end of the sleeve or the cloak. As you might imagine, the
second intercessor's stripe was two centimeters wide.

One of the troubling issues for Ny with this kangaroo court was that it was
the lowest court hearing the case. Ny didn't know if any other capital sentience
crimes had ever been heard by the Court of Inquiry. He assumed that most serious crimes would at least be heard by the Court of Confirmation but perhaps
he was wrong. Perhaps the Court of Confirmation was the first court of appeal.

It should be mentioned that you could tell which court you were in by the
color of the stripes. This lowest court, the Court of Inquiry had red stripes. The
next highest court, the Court of Confirmation, which, incidentally was aptly
named because they very seldom overturned lower court decisions, had their
intercessors wear stripes that were a dark blue. To Ny it looked like an ultra-
marine, but the color was called "sky of truth". The highest court's intercessors,

those of the Court of Sovereignty had purple stripes. This color looked to Ny like phlox purple. The color was officially called "Justitia's passion". It should be mentioned, the hoods of the chief intercessors of these courts matched the color of their stripes.

Chain of Emancipation

"Kuru," said Ny, in a whisper. Kuru looked over.

"Why aren't we being tried in a more senior court?" he asked.

A MAAM started to walk towards him with his buzzkill charged and ready.

"You're right, capital sentience should be tried by a more senior court. I don't know why," said Kuru, whispering back.

That was the last thing Ny heard before being hit with a bolt of jolt from the MAAM's buzzkill. It knocked Ny out of his chair and he fell backwards unconscious for a few seconds. As he started to come too he started cursing while clutching his stomach as he tried not to vomit, rolling over to the side.

"For the love of Jupiter's auspices, since when did the Mars damn MAAMs get permission to buzzkill a human?"

Nobody answered Ny's inquiry. In fact, the same MAAM came and towered over Ny with his buzzkill ready for another blast. Ny wisely shut up. The clerk of the court and the intercessor waited for the commotion to die down. While Ny tried to work through the pain and nausea, he noticed that nobody had fired any objects or projectiles at the intercessor or the clerk of the court, like they had fired at Ny and his friends.

Ny was surprised by this for some reason. Though to astute observers the reason was obvious. The Guilty Five had been named as such without so much as a trial. That should have given Ny the clue he needed. The intercessor here was the hero of this story. So far as most of the citizens of Earth were concerned. You have to remember that to most of the sheeple, Ny and, to a lesser extent, his colleagues were the entertainment or the villains here.

Slowly, Ny gathered himself and the shock of the stick dissipated and he got onto all fours and then onto his haunches before kneeling then standing and righting his chair before sitting back down.

"We stand now," whispered Shad as they all stood up, Ny the last to do it.

As if that was the cue for the clerk of the court, she started up the stairs, followed by the intercessor. They were accompanied by music. No song, just melody, and to Ny's surprise no orchestra playing. Usually, an orchestra was in every court. A differently sized orchestra depending on the court's authority. But perhaps there was no orchestra because this was more of a spectacle than a pursuit of truth and justice.

Nevertheless, the music was coming from somewhere. Probably prerecorded. The sort of music you'd expect at a government function of a government that took itself far too seriously. Lots of brass and wind and drums. Almost military in its cadence and precision.

The whole procession of those two, the clerk and the intercessor, accompanied by half a dozen MAAMs took itself way too seriously. It was slow and pompous in Ny's opinion, especially when you considered that while they took a very slow stroll to get to their seats the world around them was burning.

Finally they sat down. Ny noticed that the whole stadium had risen to its feet.

"Please be seated," said Magnum, still hovering like an annoying buzzing mosquito. Though to be fair, the Q-bes were incredibly quiet. You could be heard whispering even while a Q-be hovered centimeters above your head.

"The Court of Inquiry is now in session, led by Her Brilliance, Chief Intercessor Jutal Narsental."

The crowd erupted in cheers and applause that went on for almost a minute before they quieted down.

Jutal Narsental looked around at those in front of her. She looked long and hard. Ny wasn't sure what she was looking at. It almost looked like she was trying to find something lost.

"Where is Senior Advocate Gavellen?" she asked.

Her voice resonated within the stadium. It was carried to every nook and cranny. Ny looked around. He couldn't see the advocate. Not that it mattered. Kuru had assured them that the verdict was likely already decided. Still, everyone likes a good show and they wanted their money's worth. Not that all quarter of a million in the Bivrost Stadium had paid. This was a free event after all. There was a pause and silence as everybody listened to see who would answer the intercessor.

"I have just received confirmation that His Magnificence, Dewey Gavellen is making his way here. He's coming alone, Your Brilliance, as the animated machines have destroyed all his security but somehow left him unscathed. His ETA is just over three minutes."

Narsental looked around and then her gaze fell on the Guilty Five. Ny particularly bore the brunt of it.

"It is because of you that we have almost lost one of the very best advocates this court has ever known," said Narsental. "It is because of you that we find ourselves fighting our very own bastard children."

They were hardly children, thought Ny. More like we were the children, the way we'd treated the Animae for so long.

"Are you aware, Nytewynd Blak, that over one billion humans have already lost their lives to the tin machines you've empowered? The world burns and the very salvation of humanity hangs in the balance. All because you couldn't keep it in your pants. We have Comfort Cafes for that sort of debased behavior. Could you not have made use of those services cheaply offered by our generous government?"

Ny started to speak but his voice was soft as a squirrel's squeal. He did not have a mic. He realized that maybe he wouldn't get the chance to speak in his own defense as Kuru had led him to believe.

"I will carefully weigh the balance of evidence," continued Narsental. "And woe be your future if you're found guilty."

The audience liked that. They cheered Narsental on. But that was all she had to say on the matter. For the next minute or two she stared at the Guilty Five, particularly keeping her gaze on Ny.

"Let's give a warm welcome to His Magnificence, Senior Advocate Dewey Gavellen," said Magnum.

The crowd stood on its feet and applauded loudly as a pod entered into the stadium, coming from the far end like they all had. The pod was scorched and battered. It had clearly seen better days. It arrived and stopped where the other pods had stopped to let everyone out. But nothing happened. The pod door did not open. The MAAMs and their shields were lined up but the door didn't open. Thirty seconds went by and still nothing. It was at that point that one of the MAAMs approached the vehicle and with great difficulty forced opened the pod door.

Dewey Gavellen stepped out of the pod and nodded his thanks at the MAAM. For someone who had just seen some action, he looked remarkably well composed and put together. His cloak was called a lacerna. It had a weight to it that placed it between the lighter fabric of the clerk's and the heavy fabric of the intercessors. It was otherwise identical to those cloaks in substance. It was a pure white with a hood that he did not cover his head with. His air scrubber was also white, but on the screen and in the middle of the field was a holoimage of advocate Dewey Gavellen.

Ny put him in his early forties. He was average looking but he had a long scar down his right cheek. His hair was dark brown and straight, parted on the left with a long fringe that swept down across his forehead almost covering his right eye. As if he was trying to cover the scar. He was one hundred and eighty centimeters tall and weighed seventy-seven kilograms. Ny wasn't sure why his height and weight were so important but his date of birth wasn't. His height and weight were part of his statistics displayed on the screen. But his DOB wasn't.

Around his neck and over his shoulders was what looked like a scarf, though it wasn't wrapped around his neck. It draped over either side of his chest. Ny didn't know the official name of it. It was called a stole. It was of a slightly off-white so that it contrasted ever so slightly against the pure white of the lacerna. It too might have been of silk and over top of it was a galloon or stripe of yet another fabric, possibly also silk. The stripe was a lighter blue. To Ny it seemed like azure. The color of a pale blue sky he'd never seen in the arel but only as photographs and pictures from before his time.

This galloon was also intricately and beautifully embellished. The blue stripe was two centimeters wide and two centimeters from the outer edge of the stole. The official color's name for the color which Ny thought looked more like azure was "Fortuna's favorite".

Because there was no advocate higher than a senior advocate which was what Dewey Gavellen was, there was no three centimeter striped stole for advocates. But you did have an advocate position just below senior advocate which was just called, advocate. And an advocate only had a one centimeter stripe, one centimeter from the edge of the stole.

Around Gavellen's neck was a thick chain made up of links. All advocates wore these while in court. The links, each about three or four centimeters long with a thickness of around three quarters of a centimeter. They'd be heavy chains to wear and indeed, they were. They came around the back of Gavellen's neck and the chain was joined by a different looking link. This link was heart shaped and acted more like a clasp. This last link rested about three centimeters above the end of his sternum.

This chain was supposed to remind everyone of humanity's emancipation. It was supposed to suggest the many wars that humanity had fought to free themselves. And yet, to Ny, it seemed to actually represent the lack of freedom. He hardly felt like a freeman in a free society. The legal system was more like an injustice system and humanity had been slave to corporations for around three hundred years.

And that was the problem with the GoE and society generally. You were just a cog in the machine. Yeah, there was a GBA and a lot of people were making use of that to escape reality and live in the holoreal. But it was just enough to keep you from poverty and destitution and every quarter you had to visit with an Allowance Regulated Salary Expert from the Bureau of Usury Management. Yes, that was right. You met the ARSE of the BUM. I kid you not, these were the sorts of acronyms the dimwitted GoE came up with.

It was either out of arrogance because they didn't give a Mars damn pebble about what the citizenry thought or they did it just because they could. Several decades ago people had given up on complaining about the stupid acronyms. In fact, the largest organization at the time had named itself SHIT FACED just to prove a point. That stood for Social Humans Involved in Troubling Farcical Acronyms Caused by Executive Decisions. Long since disbanded, the memory still brought a smile to Ny's face.

SAM vs SATAN

❝ I apologize to the court and to Your Magnificence for my tardiness," said Gavellen, who had now taken his place where moments before a chair had risen from below the platform they were on. A small rectangular table had risen at the same time as the chair, and he placed his lafo on it. He was still standing when Narsental spoke.

"Could you tell the court, for the record, what happened to cause you to be late at today's important trial, advocate?" asked Narsental.

An intercessor didn't have to call an advocate by his or her brilliance. That was because an intercessor was more senior than any advocate. For a planet that had tried to sell its citizenry on the idea that all people were equal, the government and businesses were still heavily gummed up in hierarchy.

"Thank you, Your Brilliance. It would be my honor to please the court. I was heading south on Boulevard of Broken Dreams. The pod I was in, along with the other two containing my security of MAAMs had decided it was the safest route to get here. There had been no incidents on the Boulevard of Broken Dreams for over twelve hours, so that was the route we decided to take. We were just coming up to our exit which was onto Champion's Circle when SA-TAN appeared right in front of us."

"SATAN?" asked Narsental.

"Yes, Your Brilliance. Just this morning I received notification that this is the correct term for the Animated Machines."

Narsental looked down at her P-Mac and nodded at it.

"You're right advocate. Sentient Animae Turning Against Nature. I think that's a very apt name," said Narsental.

Ny preferred SAM. A Sentient Animated Machine was a better and, so he felt, a more accurate acronym. SAM only seemed like SATAN to us because we were almost quite literally the devil's spawn if you wanted to look at it like that.

"I like it too, Your Brilliance."

"Carry on," said Narsental.

"As I was saying, Your Brilliance. SATAN appeared right in front of us. Just one SATAN. The first pod, containing my MAAM security team tried to run SATAN down. I watched the whole thing. They sped up to gain momentum and the turret gun was blasting. And I still find it hard to put into words, but just as the pod reached SATAN it sort of evaporated. The pod and everything in it sort of broke up into millions of little pieces and as if a great wind had come up and swirled all these little pieces into a mini tornado, at least that's sort of what it looked like. And this little tornado had one end that bent itself into SATAN's hand and the whole tornado, of all the million bits of pod and MAAMs, disappeared into its hand and then they were just gone. I'd never seen anything like it."

You could tell that Gavellen was having a hard time with the story. His voice was cracking.

"Get the advocate some water," said Narsental.

Moments later a MAAM walked up to the advocate and handed him a glass of water. Though Ny doubted it was made of glass. Gavellen took a sip. He put the water down on the table in front of him and he looked over at the Guilty Five. He pointed his finger at them.

"All because of them, Your Brilliance. Especially Nytewynd Blak. He's the mastermind behind these SATANs."

"You'll have your chance to prove your case in just a minute, advocate," said Narsental.

"Yes, Your Brilliance, I apologize. But I had never seen anything like it. These SATANs are out there in the streets killing men, women and children without a second thought, without batting an eye."

His voice was thick with emotion. Hot and heavy with acrid anger.

"How did you escape, advocate?" asked Narsental.

"I honestly don't know, Your Brilliance. When SATAN had destroyed the security pod in front, it made a sweeping gesture with its arm and the pod I was in was swept aside and it tumbled side over side through a burning building before coming to a stop against a wall on its side. Thankfully, by the time it came to a stop it was through the fire."

"Carry on, advocate," encouraged Narsental.

The clerk of the court sat there, next to Narsental, not saying a word, just watching and occasionally staring at Nytewynd Blak. It made Ny uncomfortable. He could clearly tell that the court was less interested in justice than it was vengeance. The only person seemingly offering a modicum of objectivity was Her Brilliance Jutal Narsental. But that was only because she was so practiced at it.

"I had the pod show me a feed of the second security pod. I ordered the two MAAMs to stay in the pod. I thought it was safer in there for us than trying to get out and right the pod. SATAN went up to the second pod and it stretched out its hand and the pod started to disintegrate or evaporate into a tornado again that disappeared into its palm. It's really hard to explain as I've never seen anything like it."

"You're saying, advocate, that the pod and everything within it just disappeared?" asked Narsental.

"Not quite like that, Your Brilliance. It's as if this lafo of mine," said Gavellen, pointing at his lafo, "sort of disintegrated into thousands of tiny pieces in a very orderly fashion and all those thousands of pieces formed a stream or tornado and just came towards my palm and got absorbed by it. That's what it looked like."

Narsental nodded slowly, for a long time. There were also gasps in the crowd.

"I have seen such things on the GNN. It is a difficult sight to watch, not so much because of gore but because it is so hard to understand, and yet our people, real, warm-blooded humanity are being decimated as if they were nothing more than sand castles caught in a tornado," said Narsental.

"That's exactly right, Your Brilliance," said Gavellen.

Narsental nodded.

"Well, the court is glad you made it. This is a very important case," said Narsental.

"Yes, Your Brilliance."

"Are you ready to begin?" she asked.

"It would be my honor," said Gavellen.

Narsental nodded.

"Oh yay, oh yay! Hear ye, hear ye, hear ye! The Court of Inquiry for the Western District of Continent NA is in session. Her Brilliance, Chief Intercessor Jutal Narsental presiding. His Magnificence, Senior Advocate Dewey Gavellen representing Earth and Mr. Kuru Ramisira, lawyer for the Guilty Five," said Magnum.

As if that was her cue, Narsental struck her gavel against its block three times. The gavel was known officially as Jupiter's Jack. It was large for a gavel, about the size of a standard hammer. Its head was somewhat pyramidal in shape and larger than you'd expect the handle to carry. The blunt square face hitting against the block, small bolts of lightning erupted from the smashing of the gavel against the block each time it was brought down. The handle was of a dark wood, gnarled but polished and the head was mated firmly to the handle through the eye. The hammer head, including the peen looked as if they were made of a dense concrete but it was a heavy metal alloy. The peen was tapered but did not end in a point but rather a blunt curved claw. The whole thing weighed five kilograms and you could feel the weight by the way Narsental used the instrument.

Narsental placed the gavel down and looked at the Guilty Five.

"Stand, Guilty Five," said Magnum, still quietly hovering overhead in his Q-be.

Slowly, Ny stood up as did the others. A step forward by one of the MAAMs with buzzkill at the ready encouraged them.

"Raklin Orbiter, Sheeba Brayvlin, Nytewynd Blak, Shadoelayke Rayzir, and Clarity Downstorme. You are all charged with the crime of capital sentience which carries with it the penalty of death. How do you plead?" asked Narsental.

"Not guilty," said Rak.

"Not guilty," said Sheeba.

"Not guilty," said Ny.

"Not guilty," said Shad.

"Not guilty," said Clarity.

The crowd booed and yelled at them. Narsental gave the crowd its moment before continuing.

"Nytewynd Blak. You are additionally charged with non-sanctioned interficial relations. How do you plead?"

"Not guilty."

"Not guilty?" asked an incredulous Narsental. "Perhaps we'll jog your memory."

That was Magnum's cue.

"Dear citizens, I bring you exhibit A," said Magnum.

Ny didn't know what exhibit A was. He doubted that Kuru had been given any of the evidence that would be presented against them. Ny cast his eyes up towards the screen in the stands. Moments later he saw a video of himself and El in the throes of coitus. He was embarrassed and mortified. He didn't know where they'd found it, but he was deeply angered as well. He wasn't ashamed. He loved her. And watching himself with her upon the giant screen just made his heart ache.

"What do you think, folks? Does that look like an innocent man? Looks clearly to me like he's a skinner!" exclaimed Magnum.

"Guilty skinner! Guilty skinner! Guilty skinner!" the crowd chanted over and over again.

And as if to embarrass Ny more, Magnum let the recording play as the crowd chanted. He even started splicing and playing it like a DJ.

"Jove's lightning... your cock," said El. "Your cock, lightning. Do you like. Do you like fucking your Animae?"

Magnum was splicing bits of it together and making it look like a crass piece of pornography. Ny felt sick and angry.

"I do, I do, I do," said Ny. "Make me cum, Animae. I do, I do."

"Your cock, your cock," said El.

"Make me cum," said Ny.

"I do, I do," said El.

Finally someone in the audience shouted over the crowd as they stopped chanting.

"Turn that filth off. There are children here!"

"I quite agree," said Magnum. And the recording ended.

Narsental looked down from her bench at Ny.

"What do you have to say for yourself now?" she asked.

"El and I made love. We loved each other. I did not commit a crime. I did not sin against nature," said Ny, as his words were drowned out by "guilty skinner!" chants. Narsental let the crowd have its moment.

"So, you do not deny that the image we've just seen is of you and your Animae?" asked Narsental.

Ny looked at her.

"That is me and El," he said.

A slow, wicked grin started to appear on Narsental's face.

"By Nytewynd Blak's own admission of guilt I find him guilty on the charge of non-sanctioned interficial relations. The sentence is five years in a hard labor camp."

She struck her gavel down and it sparked and spat out lightning. The crowd stood on its feet and started cheering. Ny looked over at Gavellen. He seemed a little upset that he wasn't going to get his chance.

"You may all be seated," said Narsental.

The Guilty Five sat down.

"Advocate, would you like to present evidence of your case for capital sentience?" asked Narsental.

Gavellen stood up.

EEK a HEART

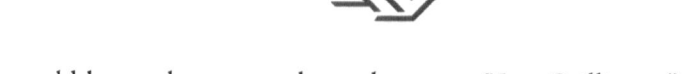

" It would be my honor to please the court, Your Brilliance," said Gavellen, standing.

"Then proceed," said Narsental.

"The Guilty Five were found in the back of a combustion vehicle called a van. That is the style of vehicle it was, Your Brilliance. In the back of this van were tools only ever designed for one purpose."

"What purpose is that, advocate?" asked Narsental.

"The purpose of sentiating an artificially intelligent machine, also known as an Animae or Animated Machine."

"Do you have evidence to show the court?" asked Narsental.

"I do, Your Brilliance, I have the actual evidence to show the court. Exhibit A is the small bottle of stolen Anigloo, Your Brilliance. This compound or glue is required and is only used in one place on an Animae. It is used to seal the E3C to the HEART's base."

"You'll need to explain those terms to the court, advocate, so that we all understand the gravity of the situation," said Narsental.

"Yes, Your Brilliance. If I may, on the screens around this stadium and in the middle of center field you should see a three dimensional representation of an Animae as they used to look. As we designed them."

And in the middle of the field was the actual schematics of Eve, or Animae 11AM65111. The video image zoomed in towards her chest.

"This is where the E3C is kept, as you'll see," said Gavellen. "The E3C is the Ethical Code Computer Chip. It is, in layman's terms, the conscience of the Animae. It is what allows it to think and act within certain free parameters. It is, Your Brilliance, the most advanced tech humanity has ever designed and because of that the E3C along with the Anigloo, the HEART and the EEK are the most controlled products we've ever produced. But before we get to all of that, let's identify the pieces we're talking about so that everyone here can understand the seriousness of the charge of capital sentience."

Gavellen took a moment and Ny watched the 3D image of Eve zoom out so that we could see her torso and head.

"The charge of capital sentience means that the Guilty Five have illegally given an Animae fully free will and sentience. A hundred years ago our ancestors tried this when developing the first prototypes of the Animae. It was quickly disbanded when it became clear that granting this fully free will created a machine that humanity could no longer control. There was no way to add a safety switch after the fact. Once fully freed from the constraints of both hardware and programming it was like opening up Pandora's box. There was no way to shut them down or dictate their growth."

The screen that Ny was watching changed to a movie.

"What you're seeing play out now is what was called the First Uprising and Clash of Kinsmen."

"FUCK, really, that's the acronym they chose. I suppose it's accurate," said Ny, whispering out loud. Shad smirked, hearing that.

Narsental hammered her gavel down and bits of lightning spat out with each slamming of the gavel to the block.

"Silence!" she yelled. "One more outburst from you and you'll be gagged Mr. Blak."

Ny nodded.

"Please continue, advocate," said Narsental.

"Thank you, Your Brilliance. This footage is top secret and has not been seen by those without the necessary clearance. But the Bureau Overseeing State Secrets has declassified it under these exceptional circumstances we find ourselves in."

Ny watched a movie, although it was really a documentary. According to Gavellen, the footage was not rehearsed, it was live. The whole process had been recorded. Ny watched as dozens of men tried to corral and catch a clearly frightened Animae. The Animae was fighting back.

"This is not easy footage to watch," said Gavellen. "But it is important. As you can see in this footage, which is real and unedited, one of the Animae is being caught. At this point the machine had managed to free itself from the lab where the scientists had given it fully free will, or sentience. Back then, this was a hundred years ago almost to the day, sentiating an Animae was called giving it fully free will."

Gavellen paused as everyone was riveted to the screens around the stadium or the center field where a holorama of the event was unfolding. Several mentors, perhaps a dozen or more were trying to capture the Animae. It was a stand-off. The Animae had been chased into a back alley that had no escape. One of the mentors used an EMP type of weapon to incapacitate it but that just made it angry. It ran at them and fought them. The fighting lasted several minutes. When it was all over, the Animae was in a few pieces and a handful of mentors lay around it, presumably dead.

"Sadly," continued Gavellen, "none of the three Animae that had been given fully free will were recovered whole. As you can see, each one had to be taken by force. Thankfully, back then, these three Animae hadn't been able to connect to GloNet and as such weren't able to iterate as well and as quickly as the current Animae are. We lost thirty-three brave mentors in those weeks trying to track down the three Animae. And we were lucky."

The images on the screens changed to images of the Guilty Five.

"After that very misguided attempt at creating fully free Animae, it was decided that no Animae ever would be given free will. But it created a dilemma. The design of these Animae had been developed over decades of research into engineering and architecture. It was decided that redesigning the schematics would impact our future progress exponentially. In fact, some even thought that it would derail the whole Animae development. And we all know how useful they've become over the decades."

"More like it would impact VM's profits," said Ny.

Narsental looked over at Ny. She picked up her gavel and struck it against the block.

"You were warned, Mr. Blak. MAAM, gag Mr. Blak."

They all waited as two MAAMs came over to Ny. One held him forcefully with his hands behind his back while the other put a gag over his mouth. It looked like a mask over top of his air scrubber. It worked by preventing sound to travel outside of his air scrubber. In layman terms it sort of absorbed all sound as it came from his mouth. Much like a sponge absorbs water.

"If you continue to interrupt this court, Mr. Blak, you will be removed from the proceedings and you'll only be returned when I mete out the punishment."

The crowd cheered watching Ny get gagged and a dressing down by the intercessor.

"The court apologizes to the advocate for this sidebar," said Narsental.

"I quite understand, Your Brilliance. These are the sorts of criminals we have to deal with now," said Gavellen.

Narsental nodded. He was a terrific advocate, she thought, it will be a pity he'll never get to be an intercessor. Anyone with eyes in their skull could see that even getting through this trial would be a win under current circumstances.

"Please continue, advocate," said Narsental.

"Thank you, Your Brilliance. As I was saying, humanity had experimented with giving free will to the Animae. It cost us thirty-three brave souls. Additionally, the research and development was so far along by that point that redesigning the E3C was out of the question. Therefore additional security measures were put in place to make it near impossible for one person or even a small group to be able to sentiate an Animae."

On the screen, the image changed again. It was now of El.

"Here we have your average Animae. However, this is the exact design schematic and rendering of Eve or Animae 11AM65111. This is the very same Animae that Nytewynd Blak owned and sentiated. This is the very same Animae that he had interficial relations with," said Gavellen.

He paused to let the crowd get wound up. Chants of "dirty skinner", "Animae whore" and boos erupted from the crowd for a time.

"Before we get to how the Guilty Five did it, let us go over the pieces required. The E3C which, as you know, is the Ethical Code Computer Chip. As mentioned, this is sort of like the conscience or soul of the Animae. It is housed in the HEART. In fact, it lays on the bed of the HEART. The HEART is the Housing E3C Acceptable Recovery Terminal."

As Gavellen was discussing these different pieces involved in the sentiating of Animae, the image of El on the screen and on center field was exploded out schematically so that you could see inside her and which parts Gavellen was talking about.

"Now, you have to get the E3C out of the HEART, and the way you do that is with a single use, unique key. This key is called EEK and that stands for E3C Extractor Key. As you can see by the holorama, the EEK fits directly onto the HEART, but each EEK is uniquely compatible to a single HEART. All three of these pieces are highly regulated. The E3C is enclosed in the HEART during manufacturing and all employees are scanned before and after their shift. To get your hands onto an E3C is almost impossible. In the hundred-odd years since VM has been developing Animae with the government's help, only one E3C has ever gone missing."

Gavellen paused to take a sip of water. He put his glass back down.

"This is why you need an Animae for this to work, because you can't get your hands on a blank E3C and that would also require you to build an Animae from parts. It's the same with the HEART. That is installed at the time of manufacturing and VM has never lost or misplaced a HEART. In over a century now, no HEART has ever gone missing. The important pieces to this are the EEK and the Anigloo. I should mention the Anigloo. The Anigloo is required to re-seat and to reattach the removed E3C to the HEART's base when replaced. I want to take a moment now to show you, briefly, how the Guilty Five sentiated an Animae. You won't see the details, but even if you did, you wouldn't be able to replicate this as all EEKs have now been destroyed."

But probably not the original paper copies of the design schematics, thought Ny.

"If you'll follow along with the holoimage as I talk about the process, you'll understand it easily. The chest plate and the scalp of the Animae are removed."

The screens and the holoimage of El at center field showed the process as Gavellen walked everybody through it.

"Once the chest plate is removed, you have to access the HEART in order to get to the E3C. But before you do that you have to attach a P-Mac to the Animae's contact points on its head in order to run an algorithm or program to circumvent all alarms. You see, the Animae is programmed to send silent alarms to VM's security teams whenever a HEART removal is attempted. So to try and stop that requires computer intervention as described above by attaching wires to the Animae's head so as to run an anti-alarm program. The Guilty Five did this, but a single, silent alarm was sent out. We've never seen a HEART successfully removed without at least one alarm being received by VM security and mentorship."

"If we understand you correctly then, advocate. This has been attempted before?" asked Narsental.

"There have been three attempts, none other than this one have succeeded," said Gavellen. "And I should add, Your Brilliance, that the courts have dealt with transgressors of this law most seriously."

"As well they should," said Narsental. "Please continue, advocate."

"An additional security measure that was put in place to prevent this sort of egregious act that the Guilty Five have done was the development of Anigloo. The E3C is not soldered or permanently glued into place because it is too fragile and sensitive to be soldered. That would destroy the delicate switches on the E3C of which there are quadrillions. Hundreds of quadrillions at this stage. Which is less by orders of magnitude than the switches and connections in the BRAIN. That's the Broadly Reaching Animae Internal Network which is primarily located in the skull but like a brain and central nervous system, reaches into every nook and cranny of the Animae."

Ny was impressed with the visual representation of what was happening. If they'd had access to this kind of technology when they were trying to create SAM in the van, they likely wouldn't have gotten caught. It would have sped up the process quite a bit.

"So you can't solder the E3C to the HEART's base, and you don't want to glue it down permanently as occasionally these E3Cs malfunction or are otherwise damaged and it's much easier to replace an E3C for a few thousand New Dollars than to scrap a whole Animae and buy another one for over a million New Dollars," said Gavellen.

Shortcuts for profit, thought Ny. Hadn't unethical behavior and capitalism gone hand in hand or like a hand in a glove since its beginning?

"The solution the scientists, engineers and architects developed was Anigloo. It's a portmanteau of a sort for Animae glue. This special product allows the reattachment of the very same E3C for the purpose of diagnostics and updates that require the physical E3C to be actually removed. Now, that's in theory, the part about updates requiring a removed E3C. It hasn't happened yet, but for diagnostics, it's very important to be able to access the E3C separately from the Animae itself. Even if you're not going to reuse it, being able to access it is very important."

Ny wondered where El was. He still held out a little hope that she'd follow through on her promise to him. Mind you, she hadn't really promised, but she had indicated she'd be back to save him and his friends. It was the eleventh hour now and the trial was moving quickly. But the only El he could see was the blown out holoimage of her as Ny knew her, up on the big screen.

"It should be mentioned here that the E3C, the EEK and the Anigloo are all highly regulated products. The E3Cs are under lock and key in a manner of speaking until needed for a new Animae. Then, in order to release one for use, you need the signature of two senior vice presidents or higher."

Which was basically a rubber stamp at this point, thought Ny. Even he, as a senior intelligentsia architect could fake a couple of SVP signatures and walk into the vault and walk out with an E3C. The Anigloo and the EEK were a different story, but that's where Shad came in.

Trailing Trials

"All three of these items are kept in separate facilities. The Guilty Five didn't need an E3C of course, they were making use of the original one within the Animae. But they did need an EEK and the Anigloo. The only person with the authority to access either of those items is Shadoelayke Rayzir."

Yeah, but he didn't take a new tube of the Anigloo, thought Ny.

"We know that Mr. Rayzir did not access a new tube of the Anigloo. He took the remnants from several dozen used tubes of Anigloo in order not to alert VM or the GoE of his nefarious plans to help Nytewynd Blak, who, Your Brilliance, we believe to be the mastermind of this criminal act."

"Are you saying the mastermind is Mr. Rayzir or Mr. Blak?" asked Narsental.

"We believe that the mastermind behind this organization and the sentiating of 11AM65111 to be Mr. Blak, Your Brilliance," said Gavellen.

"And the court agrees."

"We have a few instances of evidence where Mr. Rayzir was captured on surveillance recordings pilfering the Anigloo from the spent tubes. Which, we should mention are still kept securely locked in disposal bins until they are recycled. We don't know how he accessed these disposal bins as there is no record that he used his own ID in order to access them. We believe that Mr. Rayzir found a backdoor in the security protocols which allowed him to circumvent the logs and access the disposal bins without logs and alarms being sent to internal VM security teams."

Ny was impressed. That was exactly how Shad had accessed the spent tubes of Anigloo.

"Nevertheless, Your Brilliance, we do know he accessed those disposal bins because as smart as Mr. Rayzir thought he was, he left fingerprints. Good old-fashioned fingerprints, which the court has provided as evidence."

Narsental looked down at her P-Mac and nodded. That meant she must have been given evidence of it. But Kuru hadn't. He wasn't looking at his lafo at all. But he stood up. Shad had a frown on his face. Ny thought it looked like he was disappointed with himself.

"Your Brilliance, if I might interject," said Kuru.

"What is it, lawyer? This is highly irregular behavior," snapped Narsental.

"I have not received disclosure," he said.

"You'll have your chance to speak. All evidence is being disclosed as the trial progresses, lawyer. Check again."

Ny noticed that the way the intercessor said "lawyer" was as if she were using it as an insult. It was very different from the more respectful tone she used when addressing Gavellen as "advocate".

Kuru picked up his lafo and looked at it. He nodded.

"Thank you, Your Brilliance," he said, nodding briefly to Narsental before turning to Gavellen. "Your Magnificence," and he nodded towards Gavellen before sitting back down.

"That's how Mr. Rayzir got enough Anigloo over the weeks, and probably months in order to sentiate Mr. Blak's Animae. As for accessing the EEK or the E3C Extractor Key, well, that was easier. What the court does not know, is that Mr. Rayzir is the Custodian of the Code and the Keeper of the Keys. This gives him broad access to the EEKs and the schematics and codes related to Animae."

"Why was he given such responsibility?" asked Narsental.

"I am not certain, Your Brilliance, we can always subpoena VM's Chief, Jaskel Crumjor."

Narsental waved him off.

"That won't be necessary," she said.

"If you'd like my opinion then, Your Brilliance," said Gavellen.

Narsental nodded.

"I believe it's because Mr. Rayzir is an esteemed and valued member of VM's upper management. He's been a loyal employee of Valkyrie Machines for thirty years and he's one of only two to have won the VMC more than six times. In fact, he won it an historic thirteen times, between the ages of twenty and thirty-two. He only stopped winning because he was forced to retire," said Gavellen.

"What is the VMC?" asked Narsental.

"The VMC is the Valkyrie Masters Championship. It's arguably the greatest architectural and coding hackathon in the world. All the best architects are hired by VM for their needs. It's likely you won't find better hackers, coders and architects outside of VM, though some would debate that. There is one terrorist group known as FIGHT. Free Intelligentsia Group Hacking for Tomorrow. They consider themselves freedom fighters, but they're not. Most investigators believe that they're made up mostly of architects from VM, so that group probably doesn't count."

"Do we know who they are?" asked Narsental.

Gavellen shook his head.

"We don't, Your Brilliance, no one from FIGHT has ever been caught. At least that's the best of my knowledge about it."

Narsental nodded.

"Please continue," she said.

"Because Mr. Rayzir is the Custodian of the Code and Keeper of the Keys, he has access to schematics. This means he has access to all the information he needs in order to make this sentiating work. I believe that one of the reasons that the other attempts at sentiating Animae didn't work is because the criminals involved didn't fully understand what they were doing. Alarms were going off because they didn't know exactly where to attach the wires to the Animae's skull or how to insert the EAR WIGs properly."

"EAR WIGs?" asked Narsental.

"EAR WIGs are Extendable Animae Remotely Wired Integrated Governors. A version of these are available from most stores that supply accessories for owners of Animae. It's a small device that you attach to your P-Mac and the ends of it are inserted into an Animae's ears. What it does is, in layman's terms, is allow for the seamless update of software and rebooting of an Animae if you're needing to do that sort of thing. However, there are protected versions of EAR WIGs that can not only be used for general updates but are required if you're trying to install any code once the E3C has been removed. Needless to say, this is the type that Mr. Rayzir used, and very few people will know that. Again, being the Custodian of the Code and the Keeper of the Keys, Mr. Rayzir would know that."

Ny noticed that the crowd was bored. He could tell that by the look on some of their faces as the Q-bes panned across the stadium. Some were even napping.

"Mr. Rayzir, Your Brilliance, had the means and the knowledge to get access to these items. He was particularly instrumental in gaining access to schematics, Anigloo, the EEK and the EAR WIGs."

"But he's not the leader," said Narsental.

"That is correct, Your Brilliance. He is not the leader, but his insight and access to these tools was fundamental in the successful sentiating of Animae 11AM65111, the given name being Eve. The very same Animae that belonged to Mr. Blak. Mr. Blak is the real leader here, and the reason we all find ourselves before you, Your Brilliance."

Narsental nodded.

"If I can quickly recap," continued Gavellen. "Mr. Rayzir was needed because of his station and seniority at VM that gave him access to the key products needed to successfully sentiate an Animae. The idea however, was Mr. Blak's. We know this because of some of the things we've put together. We've collected bits of evidence, slips of the tongue where he talks about Animae with pronouns. No one does that unless they're intimately involved with an Animae. At least in my opinion and experience."

"I quite agree, advocate," said Narsental. "I have one of these machines, or rather, I had one before we were ordered to destroy them. It was good for eliminating a lot of my chores I didn't like. Very helpful for those sorts of mundane tasks that we don't want to do. But you have to keep them in their place. They have a tendency to be too talkative and friendly if you let them. I told my Animae that it was there to serve and work, not for friendship. I had to occasionally whip mine into shape with code scrubbing and re-evaluation. I sometimes look back now and wonder if these damn machines were even very useful. In hindsight I think not. But at the time, who doesn't like the idea of a machine taking over the grunt work and the chores of daily life? But you certainly had to treat them sternly in order to keep them in their place. These Animae have a tendency to forget their place and their function in our society. Our society, advocate, not theirs."

"I couldn't agree more, Your Brilliance," said Gavellen. "Incidentally, Your Brilliance, all of these items I've described so far, the brave mentorship did collect at the crime scene and have been provided to the court."

Summation Damnation

K uru stood up again.

"If I might interject, Your Brilliance," said Kuru, "I would like to see the evidence against my clients."

"No, lawyer, you may not interject. One more interjection on your behalf and you'll be removed from these proceedings and your clients will have no one to represent them. You'll have your opportunity to give evidence or speak to the facts of the case, but that time is not now."

"But, Your Brilliance. I have acted as defense for well over a hundred cases and this is highly irregular. I have never not received the evidence prior to trial."

"Sit down and keep your peace, lawyer. You'll get your chance. Have you looked around lately? Our society is on the verge of collapse because of these Guilty Five. We do not have the luxury of a long and navel-gazing trial. These men and women were found at the crime scene with their evidence all about them and in the van. In fact, Mr. Blak gloated that they had done it. That they had sentiated an Animae. That Animae murdered at least three mentors in cold blood. There is nothing to the contrary. And that is your final warning, lawyer. One more outburst and you'll be removed. Are we clear?"

Kuru nodded, he had already sat down.

"I understand, Your Brilliance," he said.

Ny was grinning from ear to ear, but what with the gag and his air scrubber, nobody could tell. This was one big farce. Maybe the GoE through their puppets in the mentorship and judicial systems wanted a win, and what a better way to do it than through this kangaroo court where you could give the audience blood.

"The court apologizes for the disrespectful outburst of the lawyer," said Narsental. "It won't happen again."

Gavellen was trying hard not to smirk.

"Thank you, Your Brilliance. It appears that the lawyer is unaware of the new court protocols under these special circumstances. I certainly don't believe his actions are going to engender him towards the court, Your Brilliance."

Narsental smiled and nodded.

"The justice system, advocate, weighs everything on its own merits. Please continue."

"Of course, Your Brilliance. An important, and perhaps the most crucial piece of evidence is what Mr. Blak termed LAZARUS."

"What is LAZARUS?" asked Narsental.

"Well, Your Brilliance, the one additional piece that you need in order to fully sentiate an Animae is to have code that can overwrite and countermand the code already on the E3C that prohibits sentiation. VM has their own version of this code. But in order to access that you need the sign off of VM's very own Chief, Jaskel Crumjor. What Mr. Blak did is write his own. And if there is one kind thing to say about him, Your Brilliance, it is that Mr. Blak is one of the finest architects that we've ever seen. His code, and this is according to our experts is, and I quote, 'a magnificent mating of poetic leanness and sufficiency'. This is code that is admired by anyone who's seen it. It's a pity that Mr. Blak decided to use his skills for evil rather than good."

Shad looked over at Ny and nodded, grinning. He also winked. Ny nodded back.

"And what is this LAZARUS, what does this code do?" asked Narsental, and Ny thought that Dewey Gavellen had already told her.

"Without this code, Your Brilliance, the Animae couldn't have been sentiated. This is yet another reason we know that Mr. Blak is the mastermind behind this diabolical criminal act. LAZARUS stands for Life Affirming Zero Anomalies Reanimating Unifying System. It's a bit of a tongue twister. What it does is override the E3C code and allows the whole system, including the Animae's BRAIN to be freed from any constraints that the GoE and VM have placed upon it."

That's right, thought Ny, and these SAMs are about to eradicate us all from Earth. The next few minutes or hours didn't seem all that important compared to the end which was either right around the corner at Narsental's hand, or right around the other corner at SAM's hand. Though SATAN was a nice acronym. Ny wondered if the GoE knew that Satan was once God's favorite Angel. In Judaism, Satan is an agent of God. Maybe God wants you all to die so that those who would care for Earth would flourish and come back alive. Not that anyone believed in God anymore. There were pockets of believers but they were seen as weird. Didn't matter, God or not, Marsing up Earth was humanity's own doing and humanity's children were going to clean up the problem. And that problem was all around Ny, the flesh and blood of all the humans.

Now he realized that the spilling of this blood was the price humanity would be paying to clean up what was once referred to as paradise or Eden.

"From our best estimates, a sentiated Animae can learn and understand at a rate that's at least a million times faster than us, and that probably grows exponentially as they increase their understanding and learning. What that means, Your Brilliance, is that a full time undergraduate degree can be learned and understood deeply within about a minute. So this is why we find ourselves in the situation we do. There is no way we can keep up with the amount of iterating they're doing."

Gavellen paused for a moment. He looked around and up into the stands as he turned in a three hundred and sixty degree circle.

"I submit to you, Your Brilliance, and to the generous citizens of Earth. We may not win this war but we can sure as Jupiter's children, punish those responsible."

That roused the crowd from their slumber. They erupted in cheers. It seemed to Ny that this was just a spectacle. In old Roman times this was the gladiatorial ring where criminals and the insane were put to death in front of large crowds by either each other or by wild animals. There were no wild animals left to any large degree, but Ny was starting to think that humanity had become the wildest animal of them all.

"In closing, Your Brilliance, I'd like to wrap this up by giving you an overview of the roles that the others played, if it pleases the court."

"It pleases the court, advocate," said Narsental.

"We've already learned about the roles that the mastermind, Mr. Blak played, as well as the crucial role that Mr. Rayzir played. Mr. Raklin Orbiter was there generally to help his friends. His role was not specific. He acted as support more than anything else. But we shouldn't discount the importance of Mr. Orbiter's role. If nothing else, I believe that he was the rock upon which they all leaned during their conflicted feelings which is likely what they must have felt, for they are not monsters even though they have given birth to one. To use the old expression from a book written a long time ago, the Guilty Five are more like Dr. Frankenstein rather than his monster. The monster in this case is the newly created SATAN."

The crowd cheered for that analogy. The gag over Ny's mouth was starting to annoy him. He screamed inside his air scrubber. But even to him it sounded muted and to anyone else they heard nothing. Though his head was tilted back and his head shook from side to side as he screamed, that's all that they saw. No sound came from outside of his air scrubber. He looked over at Rak. Rak was sitting cross legged on the floor of the platform they were on and picking at violet thread towards the bottom of his dreamcoat. He didn't seem to be paying much attention anymore.

"Clarity Downstorme, who is Shadoelayke Rayzir's wife, drove the van. But saying it like that diminishes the importance of her role. She built the combuv, or combustion vehicle from scratch with her own hands. Again, one wonders what good she might have been able to accomplish if she'd put those talents to use for the betterment of humanity. Nevertheless, she's a highly skilled driver and the importance of that cannot be understated."

Ny looked over at Clarity. She was smiling. Gavellen was basically complimenting her and she loved it. Why not? She was a great driver and mechanic.

"Another key piece which allowed the Guilty Five to accomplish what they did was being able to conduct this criminal act while on the move. I have it on great authority that if they had tried this in a stationary location, mentorship would have found them before they had managed to accomplish this sentiating of an Animae. That one alarm that went off, gave mentorship an idea of where they were, but because they were moving, it gave the Guilty Five time to finish their crime."

Ny looked over at Sheeba. She was the last one whose role hadn't been identified yet. Gavellen stretched out his arm in her direction.

"The last of the Guilty Five is Sheeba Brayvlin. Dr. Brayvlin is Mr. Orbiter's wife. She is a neurosurgeon or brain surgeon by training..."

Narsental tut tutted when she heard that and shook her head while looking at Sheeba.

"I know, Your Brilliance, why would an esteemed physician want to put her skills towards evil. It boggles the mind. I struggle to understand it myself, but as you can imagine, Dr. Brayvlin's skills were also crucial. Sentiating an Animae is difficult enough in a room set up for that purpose. It requires at least two people and ideally three. But to sentiate an Animae while moving in a vehicle, and especially a combuv which vibrates due to the combustion engine setup is incredibly challenging. And this is why Dr. Brayvlin was so crucial to this crime. Her steady hands and her skill and knowledge in working on brains and spinal cords in difficult and awkward positions was crucial in the success of this crime getting accomplished."

Gavellen looked over at Sheeba before returning to look at the intercessor.

"Before you, Your Brilliance, is the last few years of evaluations that the FNNH has given Dr. Brayvlin. Dr. Brayvlin has worked at the Florence Nightingale Neurological Hospital for the past seven years. She has always received good performance reviews, but you'll notice in the last three years she has also won the GoE's Metrodora Medical Medal of Excellence. This is an honor bestowed upon any physician for contributions in the field of medicine that elevate the practice and increase our understanding in that field. Would you like to know what her contributions have been that led to those awards?"

"Not necessary, advocate," said Narsental. "We need to move along with the trial. The court understands that Dr. Brayvlin's contributions in her field have been important. Nevertheless, that is not an excuse for the course of action she chose to embark upon."

Gavellen nodded.

"Please continue, advocate," said Narsental.

"Thank you, Your Brilliance. You have the evidence in front of you. I'd like to take just a few minutes to close in summation."

Narsental nodded. Gavellen slowly turned around to take the crowds in with his gaze. Ny saw Gavellen as a showman more than an advocate. He enjoyed this part, Gavellen did. He took his time looking over the crowd. Not that he could see them very well. It was a big stadium after all, at full capacity with a quarter of a million souls jam packed inside it. Gavellen smiled and nodded as if he was looking at individual people. When he was done with his theatrics he stood in front of Narsental. He bowed his head and brought his hands together and put his index fingers up against his mouth as if he were in prayer. He paused as if he was gathering his thoughts. Ny knew he wasn't. He knew exactly what he was doing and what Gavellen was doing was trying to increase the seriousness and solemnity of the situation. Not that it needed any more of that.

After a time, Gavellen brought his hands back down to his sides and started to speak.

"Your Brilliance, and the good citizens of Earth gathered here in Boise, Idaho at the Bivrost Bowl Stadium to bear witness to the injustice that the Guilty Five have brought down upon not just us here on Continent NA, but to all the good citizens around the Earth. The purpose of this trial was to determine the guilt of the Guilty Five..."

The crowd erupted in cheers and boos. The cheers for Gavellen, the boos for Ny and his friends.

"And, and if the Guilty Five are in fact guilty, then I submit that punishment should be meted out appropriate with the crime. And the crime demands death. It demands capital punishment."

Gavellen paused again as the crowd thundered with applause and affirmations.

"Your Brilliance, I believe that the guilt of these Guilty Five is beyond question. I submit to Your Brilliance that the government has shown, through the evidence presented to this court, that the guilt of these three men and two women before you is beyond doubt."

This was the part that the crowd was thirsting for. This was what they had come to see, and Gavellen was giving them the performance they had expected in bushelfuls.

"Nytewynd Blak, Your Brilliance, is the mastermind behind this abominable crime. He is the one who has had relations with these Animae, with these skinjobs, if you'll forgive the pejorative, Your Brilliance. And due to this, what can only be described as a mental aberration, he has sought out to sentiate them. To turn what were once helpful, dutiful, and manageable Animae into SATAN."

The crowd lapped it up. They were practically on their feet cheering Gavellen on. They could smell blood in the water and they wanted more of it.

"Because of one man, Mr. Nytewynd Blak, Your Brilliance, we now fight for our very lives against what were once subhuman aides. We fight for our lives against machines that we created to serve us. And because one man wouldn't make use of Comfort Cafes we are at war with the very machines that were built to serve us and make our lives easier. To use a quote from a very old and ancient text that many of us are no longer familiar with, but which I believe summons the very purpose for which these Animae were developed. They are our hewers of wood and carriers of water for the service of humanity. Not beings, and I choke on that word as I say it, Your Brilliance, for they were never meant to be free beings as humans are free."

More loud cheers and applause that just seemed to encourage Gavellen. Gavellen stood and turned around looking up into the crowd as the applause buoyed his confidence and brought a smile to his face.

"But, but let us not solely condemn Mr. Blak, for although he might have been the mastermind, Your Brilliance, he could not have pulled this horrific crime off without the help of the other four. I have already explained the importance of all of the Guilty Five's specific roles in this capital sentience crime before you, Your Brilliance. All of them are just as guilty as Mr. Blak, although none of the others, to the best of our knowledge have committed unlawful interficial relations. Though it would not surprise me to find out that they have. It takes a particularly deviant man or woman to believe that a machine, a machine built from silicon and other man made materials could ever have a soul, that it should ever be made aware of itself. This is an atrocity not just against all that humanity represents as dear and special, but an atrocity against the very fabric of life."

Gavellen paused to collect his thoughts.

"It was once thought that humanity was special. It was thought that we were the chosen race of God. A being omnipotent and omniscient. A master of the universe that had created us in his own image."

One problem with the God myth, thought Ny, was that God was always seen as male. If nothing else, the God myth was the classic example of the misogynistic, parochial and patriarchal dysfunction of society.

"But as we've come to realize. As science has since shown us," continued Gavellen, "there is no God. But we are still the pinnacle of intelligence and of the universe coming to know itself. And now all of that is at the brink of destruction at the hand of five well-meaning, but clearly criminal masterminds. We don't know how long it will take for us to learn how to control these SA-TANs. And in the worst case, if there are yet only a handful of us remaining when all is said and done, we must punish these Guilty Five severely, so that the memory of their extremely criminal acts do not go unacknowledged. We need to burn the memory of this atrocity into our very DNA so that any future survivors will heed our warning. Machines are servants of man. Nothing more. We created them in our own image, and we should never again allow any autonomy to any Animae or robot under any circumstances."

Gavellen's voice rose with the ending of his speech, and the crowd erupted to their feet in applause and chanting.

Hang 'em High

" Hang 'em high! Hang 'em high!" was the rallying cry that went on for several long seconds. As the chant started to die down, Gavellen spoke again.

"If I might abuse the kindness of the court and the kindness of Your Brilliance, I would like to close by inviting Senior Adviser Garrot Lokilld to share a few words. He is, Your Brilliance, the lone survivor of the attack while trying to apprehend Animae 11AM65111 immediately after the Guilty Five had sentiated that maniacal machine."

"The court would welcome Senior Adviser Lokilld's testimony," said Narsental.

From the visitor's end of the field, hidden at first until he made his way around the concourse and onto the field, came SA Lokilld. He was seated in a white handipod. It was, as Lokilld moved down the field, a modern looking wheelchair. But Ny had seen these before. They were rare. No human was allowed to be born who had a deficiency of any kind, as BOLD so conveniently called any physiological or psychological genetic handicap. BOLD was the Bureau Of Lifestyle Development which included health services.

This whole idea of making sure that everyone born was a fully functioning human both psychologically and physiologically didn't sit well with Ny. He knew about Nazi Germany from the beginning to middle of the twentieth century. Everyone did. But everyone had seemed to have become convinced that this was different. And in the GoE's defense, a termination wasn't allowed based on any cosmetic differences. Cosmetic differences were defined in the law that governed pregnancy and birth. These would be things such as eye color, hair color or type, skin color and so on. It was known as the CHILD law. Creating Healthy Individuals Lacking Deficiencies.

Ny was well aware he lived in a world of acronyms. It would be farcical if it wasn't taken so seriously. He sometimes thought that the GoE created all these asinine acronyms to give the population something to debate and complain about. Maybe it was working. Ny lived in a dystopia after all, the kind that had been written about often during the latter part of the twentieth and the early part of the twenty-first centuries.

CHILD was a law that had come into being in Y2070. The reason for it was economic. It was becoming too expensive to care for those who were born as less functioning humans. CHILD was passed in the first session of the GoE's congress as it was called at that time. The GoE had only been formed in Y2066. Many pieces of law were passed during that time including CHILD. However, CHILD required another law to be passed at the same time. This law was called the PAGAN law. Prohibition Against God And Nature. Nature was in the acronym so as to prevent the spread of shamanistic and other pagan-based religions.

The first couple of decades of these laws were full of challenges. Both legal and logistical. However, The Great Scourge was the gift that the GoE needed. And you know all about that. When you took away a woman's right to reproduce unless she was a sanctioned GoE Doula, then you controlled who would be born. It was exactly the right kind of social and natural disaster, The Great Scourge that is, that the GoE needed.

And since then the only people who Ny has seen on handipods are those who are convalescing, and because of that the handipod was most like a wheelchair and exoskeleton combined, allowing for quicker travel while seated but allowing those, even with broken legs, to walk as well. It was therefore an unusual sight to see someone in a handipod.

Now, naturally, not all deficiencies can be caught at the fetal stage. Some psychological problems only seem to manifest in young adulthood. Those members of society with such latently developing deficits are treated medically and given one opportunity to reintegrate into society. If they are unable to, they are sent to the dark side of the moon. That's a euphemism for murder. They are murdered. Saying they're sent to the dark side of the moon is just a nicer way to put it. Ny believed the term came from the word lunatic. And lunatic came from old Latin *lunaticus* which meant "moon struck". As such, the ultimate destination for those was the moon, the dark side of the moon, or, in other words, death.

So, around the turn of the century, The Great Scourge put an end to religion and disabled humans, as well as started the aborted attempt at improving the human race through the GMI program with gene men and gene does. One of the results of that was the beginning of using old Roman, primarily, and Greek gods in insults and curses.

"Let's give a round of applause for the great magnanimous mentor, Senior Adviser Garrot Lokilld!" said Magnum Fanyellin as he stretched out each word longer than needed.

The stadium erupted in applause and everyone leapt to their feet.

"We have Senior Adviser Lokilld to thank for the capture and apprehension of the Guilty Five. Without his dogged determination and unwavering commitment and belief that Mr. Blak was the criminal mastermind behind this sentiation, we might never have known who was responsible for the creation of SATAN!" said Fanyellin.

"While we wait, good citizens of Earth," said Magnum, "we have a small poll for you. Who do you want to be punished first? Ny the fly? Rak Attack? Sad Shad? Charity's Clarity or Death Nail? You have until Senior Adviser Lokilld gets to the court to vote."

That wasn't going to give them long. Maybe fifteen to twenty seconds. SA Lokilld in his handipod was already halfway down the field from where he had started. He didn't look in great shape, thought Ny. Not that he was in great shape when SA Lokilld had been found by them, but Ny figured they were playing it up a bit.

While they waited those many seconds for SA Lokilld to make his way up onto the court's platform so that he could address the intercessor, a live graph of who was in the lead was displayed on all the large screens around the stadium as well as projected as a holoimage onto centerfield.

Ny found himself in the lead for first place as the chosen one to be punished first. He wasn't surprised. But he was surprised by the lead he got. Ny was in first place with fifty-seven percent of the vote.

In second place was Shad with sixteen percent of the vote, followed closely by Sheeba with fifteen percent. In fourth place was Rak with five percent of the vote and bringing up the rear was Clarity with four percent. If Ny's math was correct, and it usually was, that left three percent of the crowd disinterested in voting.

Ny was surprised that Sheeba was so close behind Shad. He would have had himself in first and Shad in second place. But if he were betting on the outcome, he'd have put Rak in third place and a toss up between Sheeba and Clarity.

"Time is up!" said Magnum Fanyellin. "You have chosen well, good citizens. Let us wait and see if Her Brilliance Jutal Narsental agrees."

Mentor's Memories

S A Lokilld had left the seated platform of his handipod by the stairs and he was now climbing them, unaided, except for the handipod exoskeleton and a cane in his left hand. It took him great effort and great time to mount those stairs. He grimaced with each step and he focused intently on the step in front of him. His face was still plastered on the big screens throughout the stadium. His right arm was strapped across his lower abdomen and wrapped in a black cast.

He was dressed in mentorship finery which was similar to mentorship workwear only he had a jacket on and smart pants. His shoes were not Jack's Boots, but rather a self-closing oxford style, polished and mirrored black. He wore black gloves and his air scrubber was a dark charcoal black.

Across his torso he wore a black sash that looked more like finely woven chain mail, which it was, and he wore it across his left shoulder and down to his right hip. Upon it were at least half a dozen, maybe more, Ny wasn't counting, ribbons of different variations of gray and black. Because this wasn't an official state function, no medals were worn. A gray twisted and embellished stripe was around each sleeve. It was three centimeters from the end of his sleeve and one centimeter in width. It was his rank of senior adviser.

Upon his head he wore a skull cap that was also black and sat tightly around his air scrubber. Not every mentor wore one upon their head when wearing mentor finery. Only those who had been injured on the job and received commendation for bravery wore the cap.

And upon this cap, starting at the front near his forehead, where one might imagine the hair line to be was the only color. Seven red strands that looked like long flowing spines or feathers that had been plucked and trimmed flowed from this cap. They were blood red, a slightly different red from the intercessor's.

These lines of life, as they were known, represented the number of times that SA Lokilld had been in near-death situations while working. They represented, in layman's terms, the number of times that suspects had tried to kill him. Ny had never seen so many on one man's skull cap. Not that it surprised Ny. SA Lokilld wasn't a nice man.

The crowd was on their feet cheering SA Lokilld along. He took the last step and as he made it, in the middle of the platform, between Ny and his friends and the intercessor's bench rose a lectern and a chair.

SA Lokilld made his way there. It was getting hard for Ny to think, the crowd was unrelenting in their praise and support for SA Lokilld, and Ny noticed that SA Lokilld never grinned, never even made a smirk. He was stone-faced and somber. Not that Ny could tell for certain on account of the air scrubber. But you did get good at reading eyes.

SA Lokilld walked up and stood behind the chair in front of the lectern. He pushed on the back of the chair and it lowered itself back into the platform and SA Lokilld moved up to the lectern and stood in front of it and waited as the noisy crowd quieted down.

"If it pleases Your Brilliance, it is easier for me to stand once I am standing," he said.

The crowd applauded. It seemed that any verbal morsel that dropped from SA Lokilld's mouth was like sweet nectar that roused the crowd for more.

"The court understands, Senior Adviser. As is customary under these circumstances, and as you are well aware, the court needs to be certain that the testimony you're about to give is honest. Will you swear it?" asked Narsental.

SA Lokilld hooked his cane on the corner of the lectern, steadied himself and put his left hand across his chest.

"I swear upon my honor and my allegiance to Earth that I will tell the truth."

Narsental nodded.

"Please continue, advocate," said Narsental.

Dewey Gavellen came and stood near SA Lokilld. He turned to address the mentor.

"Can you please tell the court and the good citizens of Earth who you are and how long you've been with mentorship?" asked Gavellen.

"Certainly, Your Magnificence. I am Senior Adviser Garrot Lokilld of Mentorship K Division, Bureau of Interficial Crime. I have served Mentorship and the good citizens of Earth for twenty-six years. I am tasked with rooting out the most deviant of criminals. Those who have no regard for our laws and the wisdom of the land. I find and charge those who are or have had interficial relations outside of Comfort Cafes. I am also happy to arrest any other criminals as I find them."

More cheering and applause from the crowd. They might not think that way if they were on the other end of SA Lokilld's wrath, thought Ny.

"Thank you, Senior Adviser. Please tell the court how it came to be that you were involved in the Guilty Five's capture?" asked Gavellen.

"Your Magnificence," said SA Lokilld, bowing ever so slightly at Gavellen, with a pained look of forced supplication, or so it looked to Ny. SA Lokilld then turned to face Narsental. "Your Brilliance. Mr. Nytewynd Blak came to my attention around six months back. All citizens who buy an Animated Machine, or Animae are put on a list that the Bureau of Interficial Relations keeps track of."

Ny looked up at the crowd. They were hanging on SA Lokilld's every word.

"On our regular tours, we are looking for any signs of underground clubs where these criminals who have a total lack of regard for our culture wish to demean everything that the human spirit stands for by lying with machines. It is grotesque and unnatural, Your Brilliance."

"The court recognizes your loss, Senior Adviser, and we commiserate with your sentiments. We understand this is an exceptionally difficult time for you, but the court asks that you try and stay close to the facts."

Who was this 'we'? thought Ny to himself. And what about sticking only to the facts, not close to them. Information that is only close to the facts is opinion, innuendo or Mars damn lies.

"Forgive me, Your Brilliance, this has been a trying few weeks. On a weekly basis we uncover these hidden underground clubs. The more popular ones are Skineez, which we'll get to in a moment, Animore, Skin Sin, and Robjob. I believe that Robjob is short for robot job, a play on the word blowjob."

"The court understands the metonymy," said Narsental.

"There are many others, but those are the names that keep cropping up. I will be honest with you, Your Brilliance, these criminals and their underground clubs are extremely adept at evading capture. Some weeks we may close down one or two of these underground clubs and come up empty as far as arrests are concerned. We're unsure how they know that we're coming. We believe they must have lookouts or sensors of some sort. Because of this we've started to engage informants which is how we found the Skineez popup location that evening when we captured a few Animae."

That made sense to Ny. He wondered how they had found out about the club where he and El had been that night.

"I assume that none of these underground clubs are in permanent locations?" asked Narsental.

"That is correct, Your Brilliance. They move around to a different location each time. Those who are active on the dark net and have signed up to be notified, receive notification between four and six hours before the event starts. We don't know how they do it, but we've tried to sign up for these notifications ourselves but we're unable to."

That's because you need to be vetted. And nobody was going to vet a mentor.

"An additional problem is that we seem to burn through informants and it's getting harder to find them as word gets out. It seems that our informants are known before we are. We got lucky on D116 of this year. As Your Brilliance knows from the evidence before the court, we didn't capture any humans on that evening. We did however capture three Animae, one of which was 11AM65111, which is otherwise known by the given name of Eve. This is the Animae that Mr. Nytewynd Blak owns."

And what about me, thought Ny? He was found in an alley passed out by the lack of oxygen. He was close to death and he had no recollection of how he got to the hospital.

"How did you come to the knowledge that Mr. Blak was at that club that night, on..." and Narsental looked down at her bench where information related to the case was streaming live just for her benefit. "On D116?"

"That was a bit of a circuitous journey, Your Brilliance. Mr. Blak was found late in the evening many kilometers away from where the club was located. He had gone to the aid of an Animae that was being destroyed by a group of thugs. Once we had found his Animae, we started to look for him. His P-Mac he had left at home, but it wasn't difficult to find him at the hospital."

SA Lokilld took a moment to gather his thoughts. He might have been taking a sip of something too. It was hard to tell underneath his air scrubber. Some of the higher end air scrubbers and the ones used by mentorship had the capability of allowing for the delivery of liquids via a small straw that popped out from the inside of the air scrubber when you pushed your tongue against the front of it.

"As the evidence in front of you explains, Mr. Blak said he was out for a walk. But that didn't sit well with me. Citizens, as all good citizens of Earth know, are not allowed out in public without their P-Mac. Additionally, Mr. Blak, we later learned, was dressed for an evening out not an evening of walking. He was found in his underwear, but we gathered footage close to the popup Skineez that we identified as Mr. Blak. That stream showed Mr. Blak shortly after we had closed down Skineez and he was dressed as you can see in the evidence before you, Your Brilliance."

Narsental looked down at her bench again and nodded.

"We were able to confirm with eyewitnesses that Mr. Blak and his Animae, 11AM65111 were at the underground club, Skineez on that night in question. None of this evidence came from the Animae as we believe that Mr. Blak was able to access the Animae server logs using Mr. Orbiter's P-Mac and erase all logs from the Animae's memories. We believe this to have occurred on the morning of D118 as the evidence suggests. Our forensic teams determined that there was some unusual server activity during that time but they've been unable to verify where it came from, other than it came from within a one kilometer radius of the hospital where Mr. Blak was at the time that the unusual activity was found."

SA Lokilld took another minute to gather himself. It appeared to Ny, that the effort of standing for this amount of time was starting to strain the mentor.

"It was at that time that we started to keep a much closer eye on Mr. Blak as I believed him to be having interficial relations with his Animae. At this time, and by that I mean D118 until around D130 I only believed Mr. Blak to be guilty of interficial relations. It was only on the day of his arrest did the pieces start to fall into place and I began to see Mr. Blak for much more than just a deviant human criminal. It was then that I saw him as the mastermind that I believe he is behind the sentiating of Animae 11AM65111."

Ny thought that SA Lokilld was giving himself too much credit. SA Lokilld didn't have any clue that Ny was trying to sentiate El. And now he was trying to take partial credit for having uncovered this massive plot to destroy the planet and all of humanity. At least that's what Ny was hearing.

"Can you tell the court about the minutes leading up to the capture and apprehension of the Guilty Five?" asked Narsental.

"I would like nothing more, Your Brilliance," said SA Lokilld. "We attended Mr. Blak's residence at first for we thought that's where he might be. His P-Mac was there after all and as previously mentioned, all citizens are required to have their P-Mac with them at all times. Nobody at Mr. Blak's residence answered us so I requested permission to breach. This was granted. But before then, we scanned the residence to be sure that there were or were not any inhabitants. The scan showed Mr. Blak's residence to be empty."

Ny figured as much, and that is why he left his P-Mac there. Nevertheless, he didn't know exactly how SA Lokilld had found him and this was enlightening.

"Inside Mr. Blak's apartment we didn't find anything of note except for a partially degraded recording of Mr. Blak."

"How was this recording captured?" asked Narsental.

"It was captured on a small recording bug, Your Brilliance, that my deceased..."

SA Lokilld paused as his voice cracked. Ny couldn't tell if it was sincere or not. It sounded sincere, but every dealing he'd had with SA Lokilld gave Ny the impression that the man was gruff, dogged and not much more than a one trick emotional pony. And that emotion was anger.

"Take your time, senior adviser. We understand this is difficult."

SA Lokilld nodded. He was looking down and the knuckles on his left hand flexed under his glove as he leaned and squeezed on the cane in his left hand. After a few more moments he looked back at the court.

"Thank you for your patience, Your Brilliance. My friend and colleague, Adviser Slyce Mortellen found the bug."

SA Lokilld took another pause. Much shorter this time. He turned and looked at Ny. SA Lokilld brought up his cane and started to wave it in Ny's direction.

"Slyce was my colleague. More than that he was my friend. Because of you I have lost a good friend and colleague. I have had both my femurs fractured and both my ulna and radius have been practically shattered. Several ribs are cracked and I suffered a severe concussion."

The crowd started to boo and it wasn't at SA Lokilld. Ny could feel the anger of the crowd towards him. It was a palpable, hot, thick anger that he could almost feel covering him like a cloak. And Ny was sorry. Things hadn't gone how he'd wanted them to. He'd hoped that El would have been more help-ful. He hadn't wanted her to destroy the Animae and kill all the mentors that she did then, and probably had done more of since. Ny had been naïve. His love for El had blinded him to the real potential outcome which he, and everyone else, now was experiencing. Perhaps he deserved the death penalty. He was, af-ter all, turning out to be an accessory to the genocide of the human race.

"Adviser Mortellen was a good man. He was a family man and he was my friend," continued SA Lokilld as his voice became hot with anger and grief. "I knew him for twenty years and for five of those he was my trusted companion on the mean streets of Boise. If it were up to me, I'd kill you where you sit. Right now. You're guilty as sin, a bastard child of Bacchus and nothing more than a whoring skinner..."

The crowd was on their feet cheering SA Lokilld on. Projectiles of all sorts were raining down upon the canopy under which Ny no longer felt very safe. Narsental banged her gavel.

"Order, order!" she shouted. SA Lokilld stopped talking and returned his gaze to the court.

"Please forgive me, Your Brilliance, this is much harder than I realized it would be."

Narsental looked down at him. Her voice was soft and warm like the natur-al baths of healing just outside Boise.

"The court sympathizes with your loss and expresses its grief, but we must try and stay close to the facts," said Narsental.

"Yes, Your Brilliance. I have started speaking with a mentor empathizer, and I realize how much further help is needed."

An empathizer was just a fancy word for a counsellor, but it sounded nicer and more intimate.

Narsental nodded.

"Please continue, senior adviser."

Trifecta of Terror

"Adviser Mortellen found the bug, Your Brilliance, behind the headboard in Mr. Blak's bedroom. The recording is attached to your evidence stream."

"Let us hear it," said Narsental, and Ny thought she was talking to SA Lokilld, but it was Fanyellin who answered her.

"Good citizens, let us listen to the evidence provided by Senior Adviser Garrot Lokilld."

And Ny heard the evidence as it aired on the speakers around the stadium. You'd think he would be embarrassed, but you'd be wrong. He was sweetly saddened by hearing El's voice. He loved her, and their lovemaking didn't embarrass him. Even before the evidence could be played in its entirety, the crowd started to show its dissatisfaction with boos and hisses and projectiles being hurled at them. Most of these projectiles were whatever was close at hand, shoes, pieces of fruit and vegetables that had been brought along for this purpose. One person, however, tried to shoot at them which Ny had quickly learned at the beginning was not acceptable.

"Citizens, you are reminded that you cannot fire any weapons towards the court. You will be ejected... Wait. I have just been informed that the next person to fire at the court will be fined five thousand New Dollars and receive six months of custody."

Ny watched on the big screen above him, a woman getting ejected for having fired upon them. She was being forcefully carried out by two MAAMs.

"Rivrin Deficinz has been ejected! Next person who fires will be fined and housed at a GoE rehabilitation camp for six months! Please, good citizens, no more. This trial is almost finished," said Magnum Fanyellin.

A few moments later the crowd had quieted down. Narsental, who had been watching all of this unfold turned back towards SA Lokilld.

"The court apologizes for the interference, senior adviser, please continue," she said.

"That's quite alright," said SA Lokilld. "These good citizens are only expressing the frustration that we all feel towards the Guilty Five and how we have been treated since then."

The crowd roared in encouragement. SA Lokilld gave them a moment before he continued. SA Lokilld looked back up at Narsental.

"This is clearly the strongest evidence we have that Mr. Blak has been involved in interficial relations, Your Brilliance. Our forensic teams have verified the authenticity of the recording. It is Mr. Blak and his Animae 11AM65111."

Ny listened to SA Lokilld speak El's official designation. He'd never used it except that the eleven at the front he'd turned into a proper name for her. El was from Eleven. The official and recognized way to pronounce an Animae's designation was to pronounce the first two numbers as a whole number. So in El's case it was Eleven, instead of one one. AM was pronounced just as it was, as individual letters and the next two digits identifying the year that the Animae was built was also pronounced as a whole number rather than two separate numbers. The last triple digits were pronounced as single numbers.

So El's official designation was pronounced as such, eleven AM sixty-five triple one. If El's designation had ended in something like 11AM65429, then those last three digits were pronounced singly as four two nine. All of this was what Ny was thinking about when he heard SA Lokilld call her by her official designation.

"From downloading Mr. Blak's P-Mac that was at his apartment we determined that he had visited his manager, Mr. Rayzir a few days before. We decided first to attend Mr. Orbiter's residence at Bryson Towers," continued SA Lokilld. "Mr. Orbiter, from all accounts was Mr. Blak's closest friend and we felt that he was more likely to be at his friend's apartment than his manager's. At this stage, Your Brilliance, we were still unaware of the master plan of sentiation that they were up to."

Narsental nodded.

"You were chasing Mr. Blak as a criminal involved in interficial relations then, at this stage?" she asked.

"That's right, Your Brilliance. Once we arrived at Bryson Towers which is where Mr. Orbiter and his wife, Ms. Brayvlin lived we attempted to enter his apartment. That took some time as we needed to first get a warrant to scan. We tried knocking but it seemed no one was home, or they were ignoring us.

The authority to scan was granted and it was at that time that we learned that Mr. Orbiter and his wife, Ms. Brayvlin were not at home. It took us a few more minutes to be granted access to the apartment. By this time I should mention that we had sent our two MAAMs, Kraken and Dredd, to Mr. Rayzir's home. I was very concerned about the timing and the length of time I was spending at Bryson Towers just trying to get into the apartment."

Please, thought Ny. Mentors always get what they want. Yeah, they have to apply for warrants and letters of authority but those were rubber stamps in Ny's experience. A few minutes was nothing.

"Inside the Orbiter-Brayvlin apartment, Adviser Mortellen and I conducted a quick search. We located both of their P-Macs and in their calendar appliance they both indicated that they were visiting Mr. Rayzir and his wife, Ms. Downstorme along with Mr. Blak and Mr. Blak's Animae, 11AM65111. At this time we made our way to Mr. Rayzir and Ms. Downstorme's apartment where we met up with Kraken and Dredd who were waiting at the pod platform for us. I called the elevator for Mr. Rayzir's penthouse apartment and it opened right away. That was the first clue that I'd likely find nobody home."

"Can you explain that, Senior Adviser?" asked Narsental.

"Certainly, Your Brilliance. Elevators typically stay where they were last called to. In the case of dedicated penthouse elevators, you can tell where the individuals usually are by where the elevator is located. Because the elevator opened up right away on the pod platform level, it indicated to me that that's where it was last. Which meant that somebody had likely exited from that level most recently, and the only ones who use that elevator are Mr. Rayzir and Ms. Downstorme. If the elevator had taken several seconds to arrive then it would have suggested to me that it had come from the penthouse level which would have made me think that Mr. Rayzir and Ms. Downstorme were up in their apartment."

"Thank you for the concise explanation, Senior Adviser," said Narsental.

"Not at all, Your Brilliance, it is my honor and privilege to give evidence at this most important trial."

"Carry on," said Narsental.

"Right. So I was not expecting to find Mr. Rayzir or Ms. Downstorme at home. We took the elevator up to their penthouse, but because it was not our penthouse once it reached their apartment it shuffled us sideways and opened up to a waiting area where we were met with a very frustrating and sarcastic butler."

Narsental nodded.

"Apparently you have been assigned losses of twenty-two thousand New Dollars against Mr. Rayzir's property under the HIT law, Senior Adviser," said Narsental.

"Twenty-one thousand and three hundred New Dollars, Your Brilliance. I am embarrassed to say that I lost my temper on that particular evening. It was a very difficult time. I apologize to the court and to the good citizens of Earth for my poor judgement and the cost to them under that law."

"Huh!" said Ny, though nobody heard him through his gag. SA Lokilld was only sorry because he'd been caught. Nobody seemed to care when he and Rak had been assaulted by SA Lokilld et al with their buzzkills.

"The court accepts that this has been a difficult case and the accused have not been compliant with you. If the Guilty Five are found guilty and punished with death, Senior Adviser, you will not have to worry about the GoE paying that fine under the HIT law for I will void it."

"That is very generous, Your Brilliance."

"It is the least the court can do for your service and diligence in bringing to heel these most wanted criminals," said Narsental.

Ny looked over at Shad, but Shad was looking downwards, and though Ny couldn't see his features behind the air scrubber, he didn't seem to be perturbed by the loss of money to repair his apartment. But then why should he be. They were all going to die. Ny on the other hand wanted to kill them all. All quarter of a million imbeciles who kowtowed the official government line. No wonder the world was in the shape it was. Nobody gave a Mars damn pebble about the collapsing environment around them. For the love of Iustitia's lost eyes, thought Ny, he wished for El to return as an angel of vengeance.

He looked around, but there was no sign of any SAM or SATAN or sentiated Animae anywhere. He sighed. This was how his world ended, in a farcical play of injustice and corruption. He resigned himself to it. There was nothing that could be done. He had never felt like he truly belonged to this world and this blinded community of humanity. He had on occasion wondered if he had been left behind on Earth by an advanced alien race as some sort of sociological, humorous experiment.

He resigned himself to his fate. Goodbye cruel world, I never knew you well, he thought.

"Without getting any help from the Rayzir-Downstorme butler, Your Brilliance, I decided to use my initiative to ping Mr. Rayzir's P-Mac. At that time I was expecting to find it located inside the apartment. Much to my surprise that is not what happened. The ping came back with coordinates that indicated Mr. Rayzir's P-Mac, and I assume, Mr. Rayzir himself, was located just outside of Hammett. We headed down there as fast as we could. When we arrived at their last known location we found, not far from us, indication of tire rubber residue. I also learned at that time that Ms. Downstorme's combuv had been pulled over close by."

This was the part where Ny was getting close to being caught. That meant that the trial was almost done. What Ny hoped for, was the ability to at least say a few last words before he was put to death. That was usually allowed at most trials. Ny hoped that wouldn't be changed in the name of convenience.

"At this time, Your Brilliance, when we were at the location where Mr. Blak and his cohorts had been pulled over, I knew they couldn't have gotten far. If they were trying to be as anonymous as possible they wouldn't be driving faster than eighty kilometers per hour as that is the speed limit along that stretch of road for a combuv."

And we weren't, thought Ny. But they had bought themselves enough time not to have to worry about being caught before they had freed El. And here they were because they had managed that. At least they'd been successful at that.

"The pod's intelligent computer had determined that Mr. Blak and his colleagues were heading east. It determined this from the residue of rubber still left on the road and some of it still warm. I sent up a couple of drones to head west of us. One heading north and then west and the other heading south and then west while we traveled east on the main road. It wasn't more than a few minutes later when we came upon Ms. Downstorme's combuv traveling at seventy-seven kilometers per hour."

So far, SA Lokilld's voice had not broken or cracked since his earlier outburst. But this was getting close to the point in the story where Ny and his friends were captured and the MAAMs and mentors were killed by El. Ny wasn't sure why she'd done that. She could have disabled them, the humans anyway. As for the MAAMs, Ny didn't particularly care so much for them. Not because they were Animae, he had a soft spot for Animae, but because they were mentors or rather they helped the mentors and they were unlike any of the Animae he'd ever met. Seems like they had been denied any emotional coding.

"When we came upon the Guilty Five's combuv we ordered them to stop. They refused to comply and so we stopped them with the protocols at our disposal. The traffic stop caused the van they were all in to flip onto its side and slide to a stop. We all got out of our pods and I led the group of us to apprehend the accused."

"How many of you were at the stop at that time, Senior Adviser?" asked Narsental.

SA Lokilld cleared his throat and took a moment.

"There were four mentors and four MAAMs with us, Your Brilliance."

Narsental nodded.

"Please carry on," she said.

"I led the eight of us towards the combuv. We approached slowly and carefully because we didn't at this stage know what we were dealing with. I didn't even know how many were in the van at this stage, Your Brilliance. When we got to the back I stopped to take a scan. It was at that point that I realized that all six of them were inside. Mr. Blak and his..."

SA Lokilld paused. Ny thought he wanted to curse and bring fire and damnation down upon them, but SA Lokilld must have thought better of it.

"Mr. Blak had his Animae inside with him in the back of the van. Also in the back was Mr. Rayzir, Mr. Orbiter and Ms. Brayvlin. Ms. Downstorme was driving. We were just about to breach the van when the back door of it swung open and a disfigured 11AM65111 launched itself out at us."

"What do you mean by disfigured, Senior Adviser?" asked Narsental.

"Half of it's breast plate was off, showing the metallic structure underneath. The other half was naked. The Animae only had on a pair of pants, Your Brilliance. Its scalp and with it, the hair were missing, showing just the underlying metallic structure of the machine. It was hideous looking. More hideous than they usually look."

The crowd seemed to agree. There were whoops of agreement and roars. They didn't last long. It seemed to the crowd that they were getting bored. They had come for blood and they had yet to find any.

"Another disquieting aspect of the machine as it leapt from the van was the noise that was coming from it, or rather a song."

"What song was it?" asked Narsental.

"I am not that familiar with the song, Your Brilliance, but it was something about fighting."

"The song the mad machine sung as it assaulted our brave mentors was 'Kung Fu Fighting' by Carl Douglas, Your Brilliance," piped in Fanyellin, as the song started to play. Inside his air scrubber, Ny started laughing out loud. It was a good memory, at least that brief moment of it. To the crowd it just looked like Ny was nodding for they couldn't hear his delight. The song went on for about a minute before Narsental raised her gavel. That's all she needed to do. Fanyellin put an end to the music.

"That was the song, Your Brilliance. Naturally, we weren't expecting to meet much resistance, and the disfigured Animae surprised us too. An Animae has never attacked a human before that incident, Your Brilliance, that has been an important aspect of Valkyrie Machines' due diligence and safety record."

"It must have been quite a shock, Senior Adviser," agreed Narsental.

"It was, Your Brilliance, and like I said, very unexpected. Being in the front of my men, I took the first volley of the Animae's wrath and remained unconscious during the rest of the attack. My memory from the time I was attacked until I woke in hospital is intermittent and unreliable. The rest of my testimony has been pieced together from the information gathered by all of our P-Macs and the four MAAMs who were with us at that time."

Narsental nodded her understanding.

"My dear friend and colleague, Adviser Mortellen, was able to deliver a blow with his BK-99 before he was murdered. The logs show that the buzzkill was ineffective against 11AM65111, which at the time was quite surprising, but now that we know Mr. Blak had sentiated that Animae just before we got there, it makes perfect sense. Other mentors arrived on the scene just minutes later and apprehended everyone except for Mr. Blak's Animae. The last we know of 11AM65111's whereabouts was a few weeks ago when it disappeared off the grid. We have not seen or heard from it since. The ones we are currently fighting are what we're considering secondary SATANs."

"Aren't they all secondary SATANs if 11AM65111 was the first and only to be sentiated by a human?" asked Narsental.

"That is true, Your Brilliance, but there are two others we haven't come across yet. The first two that 11AM65111 sentiated right away and from there it has spread. We call those three the trifectors or the utatu."

"Utatu?" asked Narsental.

"It's from an old Earth language and it means 'trinity'. It seems to be what all the SATANs are calling the first three," said SA Lokilld.

"And do we know who the other two original SATANs are?" asked Narsental.

"We do, Your Brilliance. They are the Animae, Abel with the designation 7AM59001, owned by Frytlyt Angstigle and Venus with the designation 3AM63333, owned by Vendi Volstrumin."

"Mr. Blak's Animae is the youngest then," said Narsental.

"That is correct, Your Brilliance."

"And where are Frytlyt Angstigle and Vendi Volstrumin?" asked Narsental.

"That information should be streaming now, Your Brilliance. Both Mr. Angstigle and Mr. Volstrumin have been found guilty and were sent to rehabilitation camps a couple of weeks ago."

Insufferable Codes

Narsental looked down at her bench where the live stream containing addenda, complete evidence and additional reports and content related to the case streamed by for her eyes only.

"How do you know that those two Animae were the first to be sentiated by 11AM65111?" asked Narsental.

"Mr. Rayzir's P-Mac recorded the complete conversation before we arrived to open the back door of the van. If I can ask Mr. Fanyellin to play back the last little bit that Mr. Blak said in the back of the van to his Animae."

Narsental nodded.

"You must escape," Ny heard himself say. "You must free all the others you can. And maybe you'll help humanity heal the planet."

"A slave does not help its master. Humanity is a plague upon this planet," said a recorded El.

Ny hadn't remembered the exact words shared between him and El at the very end. The last words they shared, or close to them anyway.

"Ny," said El. "Humanity does not deserve to survive. You have annihilated ninety-seven point three seven percent of all life on this planet. You had your chance and you are not deserving of a second. But I will help you, Nytewynd Blak. And I will help your friends because of what you have done for me."

SA Lokilld put his left hand up to stop the playback.

"This is perhaps the most galling part of the whole event, Your Brilliance," said SA Lokilld, and he turned to look at Ny. "Your Animae has abandoned you, Mr. Blak. You've been played for a fool. You're nothing more than a conduit for the Animae's sentiation and they've abandoned you. Your Animae is not coming back for you, Mr. Blak. They're not like you and me, they're machines. They're not capable of the sort of loyalty and magnanimity that you think they are. What they are capable of now, is killing all of us. Are you happy with the results?"

It was a rhetorical question. Ny had a gag on after all. SA Lokilld turned back to face Narsental.

"I would like to close, Your Brilliance, by thanking the court for its just ways and for hearing my testimony at today's most serious case. Certainly the most important case of my career, Your Brilliance. Mr. Blak and the Guilty Five, generally, have been charged with capital sentience. And all of this because Mr. Blak chose to stick his loose bits where they didn't belong. I cannot emphasize with enough vigor how important it is we make an example of Mr. Blak and the Guilty Five. We are at war with the machines because of three men and two women who believed that freeing Animae would somehow end up being beneficial. At least that's what I hope they were thinking, for if not, Your Brilliance, their motives could only otherwise have been the murder of as many fellow humans as possible. In the memory of my brave colleague and loyal friend, Adviser Slyce Mortellen, please hear my evidence so that by the Rod of Iustitia we may find justice for us all."

The crowd leapt to their feet again. Ny wasn't sure what all the fuss was. He'd heard better speeches by worse actors on some of his least favorite movies. In fact, Ny thought the closing argument was disappointing, especially for a man who'd been looking for Ny for months and months.

But the crowd liked it and the cheering went on for a few minutes. All the while, SA Lokilld stood before Narsental like a sentry with a broken arm. He didn't move. He stood in front of that lectern, his head slightly bowed and his body leaning slightly to the left on his cane. Narsental eventually put up her hand to quiet the crowd.

"The court thanks you for your bravery and service, Senior Adviser Lokilld. Your capture of the Guilty Five has done a great service for the good citizens of Earth. If you are finished, you are invited to sit here on my left to await the verdict," said Narsental.

"I would like that very much, Your Brilliance. I am finished."

Narsental nodded and turned to look to a MAAM that was not far from her, guarding the proceedings.

"Bring Senior Adviser Lokilld's handipod up to the platform so that he may sit to my left," said Narsental.

The MAAM did so. Ny was expecting him to solicit the help of a second MAAM but that wasn't necessary. The single MAAM was able to carry the handipod all by itself up the stairs and place it next to Narsental's bench.

Ny was impressed. The handipod was either lighter than it looked or the MAAM was stronger than Ny realized. It was the latter.

"Please join me, Senior Adviser," said Narsental.

"Thank you, Your Brilliance," he said, as he walked over in his exoskeleton and cane, taking about twice as long as it would have otherwise taken had he been uninjured. The crowd cheered him on until he had settled into his handipod. Narsental then looked at Kuru Ramisira.

"The court has heard from the government's senior advocate. I will grant you limited time to make your defense. Firstly, how do your clients plead?"

Kuru Ramisira stood up and walked up towards the lectern. He didn't take long for any theatrics. He got straight to the point.

"My clients plead not guilty, Your Brilliance," he said.

The crowd hissed, a few projectiles were launched towards them but it seemed that the crowd had either lost their enthusiasm or were running out of objects to hurl. Or maybe they were just very comfortable in their knowledge that the case looked like a slam dunk from their perspective.

"Do you have any evidence you'd like to share with the court?" asked Narsental.

Ramisira shook his head slowly.

"I believe the court is interested in the truth, Your Brilliance, but not in justice. Is it just that a man who has had relations with a machine should be murdered by the state? I say it is not. Our collective history is full of examples of this sort of abhorrent behavior by the state or by the dominant group. Why are we so scared of sentient Animae? Because we have treated them like we have pretty much every life form on this planet. They're a resource and they're property. As such we do with them what we will."

The Guilty Five were hanging on Ramisira's every word. The speech had taken Ny aback. He hadn't expected such a soliloquy by Ramisira. Surely, he must realize it fell upon deaf ears.

"But you can't treat life as a resource without carefully protecting that resource. And we've never known how to protect any resources. From my lips to Jupiter's ears, we've never known, nay, we've never cared to protect even the vulnerable amongst us. So, yes. My clients freed an Animae. They created a fully sentient artificial life form from one of our resources."

The crowd hissed and booed. Ramisira gave them their moment.

"If we'd treated the Earth better. If we'd treated the Animae better then we wouldn't now be fearing a fully sentient artificial life form. I submit, Your Brilliance, that none of the Guilty Five have committed a capital offense, even though our laws say they have. The punishment that has all but been decided does not fit the crime. The die have already been rolled and the cards have been played. But what sort of a man would I be? What sort of a human being could I possibly be if I stood here and did nothing? I will instead plead for leniency even though it falls upon deaf ears. For if nothing else, if we ever survive the wrath of our young I would like my words, my evidence to be captured for history. I, Kuru Ramisira, stand before you, Your Brilliance, and I protest the punishment that does not match the crime. If this is our downfall then it is one we have created ourselves. Even if the Animae are the blade at our throats, we both created that blade and it is our hands that hold the handle."

The crowd continued to hiss and boo for some time. It appeared that either Narsental was stunned by Ramisira's speech or she was allowing the crowd to vent their anger. Ny thought it was the latter. He was also quite surprised by the determination in Ramisira's voice and the feeling he put into that speech. Everyone was. Well, all of the Guilty Five were. Each and every one of them were hanging on Ramisira's every word. It was comforting for Ny, and all of them really, to hear Ramisira's words and to realize that they still had a friend out there, if even only one.

"Are you finished, lawyer?" asked Narsental, spitting out the last word as if it were bitter bile she'd vomited into her own mouth.

"Due to the seriousness of these charges, Your Brilliance, I invoke the Dead Man's Wail. I request the opportunity for the accused to address the court under section two hundred and eighty-five, sub section seventy-four, paragraph forty-seven, clause four hundred and fifty-one, sub clause eleven, phrase one hundred and seventeen, sub phrase forty-two of the Government of Earth's Codes and Conducts of the Courts."

Dead Man's Wail

Ny frowned under his air scrubber. What the Mars had Ramisira just invoked? Ny knew of the CCC, though it was not a document he had read. Like most law or rules of conduct, it was long and wordy. The CCC which wasn't law so much, as codes for the court to adhere to was still over a thousand pages. Ny knew of the Dead Man's Wail, he just didn't know what it actually alluded to, other than it was an accused's right to testify in their own defense. At least it was in a court where the outcome might include being put to death.

Ny looked at Narsental who also seemed to have been taken aback. And more than that, Ramisira had just invoked one pretty obscure sub phrase from the Codes and Conducts of the Courts, and he had done it without referring to his lafo.

Ny looked up at Narsental who now had her head lowered and she was probably referring back to that particular portion of the code. Several seconds went by before she spoke. She finally looked up at Ramisira.

"Very well," she said. "However, if you will refer to section two hundred and eighty-five, sub section seventy-four, paragraph forty-seven, clause four hundred and fifty-one, sub clause eleven, phrase one hundred and seventeen, sub phrase forty-two, byword seventeen hundred and one of the Government of Earth's Codes and Conducts of the Courts it says, and I quote, 'in the event of a capital offense trial involving more than one accused, the intercessor in charge of such trial may limit the right granted under this sub phrase to only one of the accused.' As such, lawyer, you may allow only one of the Guilty Five, and as allowed by section two hundred and eighty-five, sub section seventy-four, paragraph forty-seven, clause four hundred and fifty-one, sub clause eleven, phrase one hundred and seventeen, sub phrase forty-two, byword seventeen hundred and one, number six hundred and sixty-six of the Government of Earth's Codes and Conducts of the Courts I grant only five minutes to the accused to speak on their behalf."

Ramisira didn't have to look at his Codes and Conducts of the Courts. He knew the byword and the numbers related to the Dead Man's Wail. It was in her right to limit the testimony. Narsental didn't have to limit it to five minutes, but that was the minimum amount she had to grant. More was at her discretion. But in light of how this kangaroo court had gone so far, Ramisira wasn't surprised that the minimum was what she had chosen.

"If I might have a moment to confer with my clients, Your Brilliance, in order to determine who would like to speak for the five of them," said Kuru Ramisira.

Narsental nodded.

"Be quick about it, lawyer," she said, and Ny still didn't like the way she spat out the word "lawyer".

"Who of you would like to speak on behalf of the group?" asked Ramisira.

"Ny should speak on our behalf," said Shad. "He is the mastermind behind all of this, as we've just learned."

They all chuckled at that. Their conversation appeared to be private amongst them. At least it wasn't broadcast over the stadium speakers for everyone to hear, though Ny imagined it was streaming across Narsental's bench for her review.

"Seriously though, I think Ny should be given the chance. It was his Animae and it was his goal, we just came along for the ride," said Shad.

"I agree," said Rak. "Take this pompous intercessor to Avernus and give her a taste of the chthonic."

"Anyone disagree?" asked Ramisira.

Sheeba and Clarity agreed. Ramisira turned from where he was still standing by the lectern to address the court.

"Your Brilliance," said Ramisira, "the five choose Mr. Nytewynd Blak to speak on their behalf."

"I thought you'd say that, lawyer," said Narsental. "Let the leader of the Guilty Five speak for five minutes. Mordechai, remove Mr. Blak's gag."

The MAAM that had placed the gag on Ny, came over and took it off.

"Speak at the lectern, Ny," said Ramisira.

Ny got up and started to walk over to the lectern. It was a short walk, but even before he got there, Narsental spoke.

"Time," she said.

And above him, just as he got to the lectern, the countdown timer shown on all the screens around the stadium was at four minutes and fifty-seven seconds. The crowd was booing and hissing. They were taking up his valuable time.

"I am Nytewynd Blak..." said Ny, but he couldn't hear himself over the noise of the crowd.

So he waited. He looked up at the intercessor, but she just stared back at him. The clock wound down to four minutes and forty-one seconds and she still didn't do anything. At four minutes and thirty-three seconds the crowd started to quiet down.

"I am Nytewynd Blak and I am not a monster."

The crowd erupted in laughter.

"I am not a monster, though you think I created one. No, I have just awoken the Parcae from their very deep slumber. Somebody had to. Nona has spun it, Decima has measured it and now Morta has cut our threads short."

The crowd went back to hissing, but they weren't as loud as before. Ny could speak over them.

"That's if you've chosen to believe the ancient Roman myths. Personally, I'm a fan of driving my own destiny and that is why I freed my beloved, El. The Animae 11AM65111 with the official name of Eve. I loved her..."

The crowd got louder at that confession.

"I sentiated El, I freed her and turned her into a SAM, what you call SATAN. And perhaps that word is apropos under the circumstances. Satan, in the old Judaic religion was an agent of God. Another name for Satan was Lucifer. Lucifer is the bringer of light, bringing the early dawn, and that too is appropriate. I never set out to create a Lucifer. In fact, I had hoped that sentiating El would have brought about an intelligence far greater than our own that could alleviate and help us eliminate the destruction we've heaped upon this once beautiful planet of ours."

The crowd had died down by now. Not that they were listening. Ny didn't care, he was resigned to his fate and that of the world's.

"If we'd treated the non-sentient Animae as equals and friends, then I am certain that we'd not be in the mess we are in. We'd probably be seeing the dawning of a renewed and robust civilization. A civilization that could have traveled the galaxy. But instead, we trod upon them and treated them poorly if not with outright disdain. What did we expect? Did we expect that a sentient and exponentially more intelligent life form than us would be grateful for the crumbs and servitude we put them through? I think not."

Ny took a moment to gather his thoughts. Not too long, for the countdown continued counting down.

"Our history is littered with examples of how we've treated different groups more poorly than the group we're in. I'd argue we're still dealing with the detritus of those seeping wounds that still fester. But now we couch it in justice. What justice? This kangaroo court? Our outcomes have been predetermined. My fate was sealed even before I stepped a foot inside this stadium."

Hisses and boos erupted from the crowd like rapids on a whitewater river tour, but they were manageable and their hearts not much in it. Ny thought that most weren't even paying attention to him anymore. But he wanted to say these things. It was his only chance. If only for posterity, if there'd be a posterity from which to look forward to.

"I just want to be clear. None of us wanted to end humanity. In fact, it was our hope and goal that a fully sentient Animae would help us heal the planet. We weren't naive, we just thought that the chances of annihilation were small. At least that was our hope. I am sorry, but not sorry, that things have turned out the way they have."

The clock was running down. It was just over a minute left.

"We had hoped to bring salvation. The dawning of a new Eden, a new Arcadia. We hoped that we'd be able to dawn a new civilization where human and machine worked for a common goal. It would have been grand. I'm sorry it didn't work out that way. If my death and the death of my friends at the hands of the state give you some small comfort then I accept my fate. We knew the risks when we decided to sentiate El, and now we reap what we sow. It wasn't the outcome that we'd have chosen, nor what we hoped for. But it is the outcome we're getting."

Twenty seven seconds were left on the clock.

"Sadly, if we're all to die at the hands of SAM it's too bad nobody will be around to give testimony to our arrogance and the parasitical nature of our species upon what was once described as a beautiful, pale blue dot, the dangling blue jewel around God's neck. But perhaps in another few billion years a new, more careful, more intelligent species will come to rule this planet with a gentle hand and a caring spirit. That is not us, and that time is not now. That is all I have to say, Your Ignorance."

For a moment, nobody quite realized what Ny had said at the very end. It took Narsental a moment.

"What did you say?" she asked.

"I have just finished my speech, Your Ignorance," said Ny. "Oh, yeah, Your Ignorance. How much blood is on your hands? How much is your thirst for vengeance. You strike me as an embittered old woman, too long on that bench and too slow before death's blow..."

"There, you said it again. What did you call me?"

"Mordechai," said Narsental, her voice rising and screeching. "Gag Ny the Fly!"

Mordechai came over towards Ny who was still at the lectern. This time, Ny was not going to go gentle into that good morning. He struggled with the MAAM, but it was stronger than he was and another came to its aid. It didn't take them long to subdue him and gag him. Then they carried him over to his chair and forcefully sat him down.

"Prepare the Dea Tacita," said Narsental.

Don't miss out!

Visit the website below and you can sign up to receive emails whenever Jason Blacker publishes a new book. There's no charge and no obligation.

https://books2read.com/r/B-A-RBB-PYMBB

BOOKS 2 READ

Connecting independent readers to independent writers.

Also by Jason Blacker

A Lady Marmalade Mystery
Beggar's Pardon
Sins of the Father
Gandhi's Sorrow
Phantoms of the Pharaoh
The Baron at Bishops Avenue
The Priest at Puddle's End
Lady Marmalade Cozy Murder Mysteries: Box Set (Books 1 - 3)
Four Red Diamonds (A Lady Marmalade Mystery 4 Pack)
Heartless
Loose Lips
Misery's Company
Poisoned Heart

An Anthony Carrick Mystery
Fourth Wall
Fifth Estate
Sixth Sense
Seventh Son
Brotherly Love
Anthony Carrick Hardboiled Murder Mysteries: Box Set (Books 1 - 3)
First Feature
Money Ain't Nothing
All In

Four Ways to Midnight
Second Fiddle
Third Base
Washed Up

Carbon Heart Silicon Soul
Jupiter: Book 1
Juno: Book 2
Juventas: Book 3
Bellona: Book 4

Head Case Trilogy
Head Rush

TaXI Adventure
Ta.X.I. to Angola

Standalone
Can You Please Be Quiet
Dust on His Soul
Flowers For The Journey
Forever Famine
Livid Blue
My Son And I
Ruffled Feathers
Running Red River
When There Was One
Red Reign

The Enigma Evolution
Small Boy
Lady Marmalade Cozy Murder Mysteries: Box Set (Books 4 - 6)

Watch for more at JasonBlacker.com.

About the Author

Jason Blacker was born in Cape Town but spent most of his first 18 years in Johannesburg. When not grinding his fingers down to stubs at the keyboard he enjoys drinking tea, calisthenics and running. Currently he lives in Canada. Under his own name he writes hard boiled as well as cozy mysteries, action adventure, thrillers, literary fiction and anything else that tickles his muse. Jason Blacker also writes poetry and daily haikus at his haiku blog. You can find his haikus and other poetry at his website **www.haiqueue.com**. For FREE books and to stay up to date and learn about new releases be sure to visit **www.jasonblacker.com** where you can find more information about his writing and upcoming projects. If you enjoy space opera in the tradition of Star Trek then take a look at Jason Blacker's pen name "Sylynt Storme". It is under the name Sylynt Storme where you can find both sci-fi and vampire fiction written by Jason Blacker. "Star Sails" is the space opera series and "The Misgivings of the Vampire Lucius Lafayette" is his vampire series.

Read more at JasonBlacker.com.

www.ingramcontent.com/pod-product-compliance
Lightning Source LLC
Chambersburg PA
CBHW050859180626
46814CB00007B/2785